ROE VALENTINE

EVERNIGHT PUBLISHING ®

www.evernightpublishing.com

Copyright© 2018

Roe Valentine

Editor: Audrey Bobak

Cover Artist: Jay Aheer

ISBN: 978-1-77339-576-0

ROE VALENTINE

ACKNOWLEDGEMENTS

Thank you to my awesome friend and critique partner, Molly Mirren, for helping me smooth out this story. I appreciate your sharp grammatical eye and insights. I am so lucky to have you! Also, thank you to my beyond amazing friend Teri Wilson for giving me a great idea for this story. You are both rock stars to me. Huge thanks to Stacey and Audrey for helping me get this story to publication. The Evernight Publishing family is a delight to work with. I thank you all from the bottom of my heart.

ROE VALENTINE

PLAYBOY BOSS

Society Playboys, 2

Roe Valentine

Copyright © 2018

Chapter One

"A-Plus Temporaries sent someone to fill in for Marisol while she's on maternity leave. The girl is waiting in the lobby." Susan, the receptionist, placed a résumé on his desk.

Fucking brilliant.

"Is she absolutely atrocious?" Konrad glanced at the bright white sheet of paper, noting only the education section. Bachelor's in Business Administration. There was no real work experience listed. *Fantastic.*

Why did his assistant have to go into labor just when he was working on an important property sale? Konrad was married to his work. No question there. But he knew life happened, and not everyone felt the same way about employment. He pushed the résumé back to Susan, who didn't take it.

With a nervous laugh, Susan said, "God, I hope not for her sake. And yours."

Konrad grunted. Incompetence was not tolerated at Korr Corporation, or in any other aspect of his life. This temp had better be immaculate.

He waved his hand. "All right then. Send her

back."

Susan nodded and moved toward the door, and then closed it behind her. Konrad watched her hips sway from side to side through the glass wall. Not to check her out, because Susan was like a sweet aunt to him, but to count his heartbeats. He didn't necessarily hate change. He simply hated losing something that worked for him. Obviously, he'd already deemed the temp a failure before she even stepped foot in his office. He also knew that wasn't fair.

Breathing in deeply, he decided to chill out. What was three months? Barely ninety days. Just twelve weeks. *Hell*.

An email notification chimed through his laptop, taking his attention. He scanned the sender's name. *Tamsin*. He sighed. *For fuck's sake*. He'd cut her loose the night before. It would have gone smoothly if she hadn't disagreed with his decision. Of course, he had to remind her they'd never been exclusive. The night they met, he'd told her point blank he only wanted a bit of fun. With an expiration date. He'd had two other women on rotation, not including the hookups he indulged in as he saw fit. With his work demands, Tamsin had become too much to handle.

Easy. Fun. Hot. Fleeting. That was how he liked his women. That was all he knew and felt comfortable with. Exclusivity and commitment weren't his game. Never had been. Pilar, his date for that evening, knew how to be easy, fun, hot, and fleeting. Plus, he was on *her* rotation of men as well. So, all was fair between them.

Konrad opened Tamsin's email, dread passing through him.

To: Konrad Korr (konrad@KorrCorp.biz)

From: Tamsin White
(Tamsin.White@huntergreenewhitelaw.biz)
Date: Monday, September 4
RE: Meeting at L'Atelier at 8:00 PM
Konrad— After last night's discussion, I would like to meet to discuss the situation further. I've made us reservations at L'Atelier tonight at 8:00 PM. I expect you to be there.
Kind regards,
Tamsin White
Junior Attorney
Law offices of Hunter, Greene, and White

Situation? What fucking situation? Tamsin did not know how to get rejected. Konrad blamed himself, though. She was a lawyer, after all. Every attorney he'd ever dated couldn't just let it go when their dalliance expired. Always an argument to be had. Always a headache he didn't need. He sighed. Some flings just couldn't leave as quietly as they arrived. Thank God there hadn't been many of those. He'd have to blackball lawyers going forward. Unless they approached *him* with an arrangement...

Just as he set his fingertips on the keyboard to type a polite kiss-off response, his office door opened. Susan and a mousy petite woman stood under the doorjamb, peering at him. At first, he was disappointed the agency didn't send over a bombshell. He wasn't a monk, after all. But he was feeling much more jerkish than usual that morning.

"Well, don't just stand in the doorway. Come in." He waved them in, a bit annoyed at the way they cowered. If this was any indication of how the temp worked, he'd need a new temp for tomorrow.

Susan led the parade of two deeper into his vast

office. "Konrad, this is Scottine Roberts from A-Plus Temporaries." She practically shoved Scottine toward the desk.

Scottine? An unusual name he'd heard only once when he was in boarding school in the UK. She was a French teacher. And very hot. He glanced at the résumé again to verify the name. *Scottine Roberts.*

"Scottine, is it?" He lifted his eyebrows for emphasis.

She avoided his eyes. "I go by Scottie." Her voice wasn't as bland as he'd assumed it would be. At least there was that. She looked uncomfortable, her hands behind her back.

He considered her, taking in her face. On further inspection, he'd decided she was rather cute in a librarian sort of way. And a touch exotic. Hazel eyes, wavy, dark hair, smooth olive skin, full pink lips. All things he normally liked in a woman. Sadly, her loose black trousers and button-up blouse didn't do much for her shape.

Making his British-German accent thicker, he said, "Okay, Scottie. You can call me Lord Korr." He held back a laugh. She, on the other hand, was deadpan.

Susan laughed. She'd always appreciated his jokes. Clearly, this Scottie Roberts had no sense of humor. Square on him, her eyes narrowed. She didn't seem impressed. A spike of unprecedented excitement worked through his body.

"He's just kidding. It's his German or British humor. I think. None of us have figured it out yet." Susan tried to lighten the mood.

Konrad waved his hand in mock defeat, still feeling the sensation of intrigue in his body. "Fine, you can call me Konrad."

The steady tingles continued to surge through him

as his gaze met Scottie's, who still did not seem impressed. No indication of interest. No beaming. No blushing. No trying to please him in anyway. Scottie might very well think he was a jackass. He zeroed in on her face, trying to find some inkling of an emotion. Instead, he admired the freckles on her nose, her thick dark lashes and high cheekbones. *My God.* She was not cute or librarian-ish at all. In fact, she was actually quite beautiful. Aphrodite could have been standing in his office.

She looked away first, though, which made him feel oddly triumphant. *She'll come round.*

Susan reminded them of her presence with her interjection. "Very well ... I'll show you to your cubicle, which is just outside. Mr. Korr...?"

"Mr. Korr?" Konrad paused. Susan had never called him Mr. Korr before. He hated to be called Mr. Korr. His father demanded it, and Konrad was not like that man.

A nervous laugh slipped between her lips. "Right. Sorry. I don't know why I'm being so weird." She glanced at Scottie, who waited intently and looked bored. "Do you want Scottie to have full access to your email?"

Full access... That was a phrase he liked on most occasions. Yes, he very much preferred full access. But Susan was talking about something very different, and he should not be thinking about full access to anything with the temp. "Give her limited access. She can edit my calendar. Make sure she has her own email address."

"The korrtemp@KorrCorp.biz address?"

"That's the one."

When he glanced back to Scottie, she'd had her attention on him. A different look in her eyes that time. Not annoyed, not unimpressed, not bored. Curious, maybe. Still not the usual interest he'd get from women.

"Come back to me when you're done getting sorted out. I want to go over some minor requirements." Konrad waved his hand at them. "Off you go."

The women left him in the buzzing silence of his office. He stared at the computer screen for a moment, discombobulated and not sure what the hell had just happened. Had she really not been dazzled by him? All women were dazzled by him. It was a fact, not anything he'd claim on his own. Seriously, this was a first for him.

An email notification chimed from his computer again, interrupting his ridiculous thoughts. He'd received an email from a potential buyer for an East Downtown Houston warehouse property he'd put up for sale. The "EaDo" property was in demand. A microbrewer, Bayou Sling, wanted to set up shop in EaDo, but Konrad had hopes for Ortho-Sync, a small medical device company, who wanted to build a manufacturing plant in Houston. If they offered him the money he wanted, he could buy another EaDo property he'd had his eye on. The thought of growing his real estate empire thrilled him.

Just then, his private direct line rang. He punched the intercom. "Konrad Korr."

"Mr. Korr, please hold for Mr. Fabian Pallis."

Konrad rolled his eyes. Fabian had only been partner at his father's engineering firm for a month, and he'd already had some poor woman waiting on him hand and foot. Not that Marisol hadn't waited on Konrad hand and foot, as would Scottie. The notion made him chuckle.

"Well, hello, Mr. Korr," Fabian said in his professional voice.

"Are you serious with your assistant calling on your behalf?"

He laughed. "I'm just having some fun."

"You better hope Antonia doesn't find out you're

using that poor girl."

"She won't find out. Besides, I think my secretary likes to be used." He laughed.

Scottie didn't seem like the type to like to be used. Why did he keep thinking about her?

"What do you want?" Konrad stared at his emails again. He'd forgotten about his kiss-off email to Tamsin. "I'm working, unlike you, I'm sure."

"Doubtful!" Fabian laughed again. "Toni and I are having a dinner thing tonight at her penthouse at eight. You coming?"

"A bit last-minute, no?" He glanced at his naked wrist, sighing. He'd lost his favorite watch. A Richard Mille that cost more than a townhome in the Museum District. Now he only had the Rolex, which he didn't care for.

"And...?"

"Fine. I suppose I could move things around." He'd have to figure out what to do with Pilar. Perhaps they'd have a nightcap instead of dinner. She liked nightcaps just as much as he did.

"Bring a date."

"Good God, mate! Just because you're coupling up doesn't mean everyone else is. You know my opinion on that." He sat back in his chair. How many times could he tell Fabian he was not interested in a relationship? Since Fabian "fell in love," he'd been impossible to talk to.

"Oh right. You believe in love, *for everyone else*."

Konrad sighed. "That's right. I'm a bachelor for life. I'm saving some poor girl from a lifetime of loneliness and depression." The word *depression* settled in his stomach, making him nauseous for a second.

"So you say."

The line was silent, and Konrad would not say another word about it.

Fabian continued when he seemed to get the hint. "Everyone else is bringing a date. Tylund and Dallas said they have dates."

Konrad snorted. Those guys *always* had dates. They weren't too different from Konrad, though he knew they'd end up like Fabian eventually.

Worst-case scenario, Pilar would meet his friends after he'd briefed her on the situation. He suspected she'd get the picture without much explanation. She was the daughter of a Mexican diplomat and knew how to behave appropriately. Thank God for noncommittal women like Pilar.

"Fine. I'll be there." Konrad disconnected the line because he knew Fabian absolutely hated to be hung up on. After springing that couples' dinner on Konrad, Fabian deserved worse.

Hell. He rubbed his eyes, feeling tired. He'd been working overtime. Keeping up with his three companies, Korr Corporation, Korr Properties, and Korr Solutions, had proved to be a challenge. Nothing he couldn't handle though. His bastard father was a workaholic. He'd learned from the best.

With slow hands, he pulled out his cell phone from his desk drawer and dialed Pilar's number. She answered on the fourth ring, just when he was about to end the call.

"Hey, *guapo*. I missed your accent."

Konrad smiled. She had her own sexy Spanish accent. And yeah, he was handsome. Paired with his German-British accent, he wasn't sure why Scottie's knees hadn't buckled upon meeting him. Okay, that was too much. Even for him. "Did I catch you at a bad time, love?"

"No. I'm just walking to class." Pilar was an international student at the University of Houston. She'd decided to complete another semester before transferring to UCLA in the spring, which Konrad was glad about. He wanted to enjoy her a little bit longer before they said goodbye. "What's up?"

"There is a change of plans for tonight."

She paused. "Okay…"

He waited, and he tried to come up with another plan that didn't include his friends. Why did he feel so much anxiety about the dinner? The issue wasn't Pilar. He knew she'd go with the flow. But his friends … could they forget her as quickly as he'd ask her to forget them?

"Kon? Are you okay?"

He looked at his computer screen, catching his reflection when the screen went black into sleep mode. *Fuck it.* "My friends, Fabian and Antonia, are having a sort of dinner party thing tonight. It's all very last-minute, but he's expecting me to go. So … I thought you'd come along with me, since we already have a date planned for tonight."

The ensuing silence made him think she'd hung up, but her choppy breathing let him know she'd been walking. "Sure."

No enthusiasm in her response made him confident that all would be well. She didn't seem to have an expectation that would worry him. "Fantastic. I'll send you a text when I'm on the way to the campus. It starts at eight."

"See you. *Ciao, ciao.*" She hung up with her signature farewell sentiment, leaving him sucking in a deep breath.

That went well. He hoped the dinner would go seamlessly as well.

Before Konrad could decide what to focus on

next, the door opened. Scottie walked in. She'd not knocked and waited for his approval to proceed. He frowned at her boldness but felt the same exhilaration from earlier. Their eyes met, hers blazing like amber fire with green flames. She had the most incredible eyes he'd ever seen.

"Konrad, are you ready for me?" She walked reluctantly to the chair across his desk, a notepad in hand.

"Sit," he said, leaning back in his chair. The sturdy back stabilized him as he watched her. She sat, her knees together and both smooth, tan hands on her lap. He noticed she didn't wear any jewelry. "We told A-Plus Temporaries that we wanted the best they had to offer. So, I expect you to be the best."

Her eyes widened. She didn't look so bold then. "Well, sir, I will *try* my best."

Her seemingly sudden desire to please him didn't satisfy him as he thought it would. Konrad wanted her to be cockier. He wanted her to tell him to piss off.

"Well, that's all any of us can do, right?" He continued at her nod. "I have the typical office requirements, such as answering my public line for Korr Properties. I also have a Korr Solutions line, which is my other company two floors down, but you won't have to do anything for that. Side note, if you aren't aware, Korr Corporation is comprised of Korr Properties and Korr Solutions. So, I have three companies total. But, you need only worry about Properties."

"Got it." She wrote on her notepad.

"So, to summarize, just filter calls to me, schedule meetings, help with presentation slide decks, compile reports and comps for properties as instructed, copying, and filing, just to name a few. Nothing eccentric, if that's what you're worried about. I will, however, need you to do … personal tasks for me."

Her eyebrows furrowed.

"Does that scare you?" *Why did I ask that?*

Scottie met his challenging eyes. "Should it?"

He chuckled. There was the cockiness he wanted. "Not at all." He'd have to think of a personal errand for her to run just to get her feet wet.

"Can you give me an example of these personal tasks? The agency has rules."

And clearly, she didn't like to break rules.

He leaned forward, opening his drawer again to fetch out a business card. "I'll do better than an example. I'll give you a task straight away." He handed her his florist's card. Yes, he had a florist. "Send flowers on my behalf. A dozen roses to two different individuals."

With her mouth partly opened, she took the card, her warm fingers grazing his, shocking his system. She glanced where they'd touched. "Two?"

Their eyes met.

"Yes. Two different women."

A look of disbelief colored her face. "Oh…"

"Will that be a problem?" He sat back again, enjoying her reaction to him. Yes, he was indeed in a jerkish mood that day.

"No, sir." Her mouth said the words, but her face betrayed her.

Chapter Two

Not one, but two women? Who the hell did this guy think he was? Don Juan? Okay. Scottie had to give it to him. He was way above average in the looks department. And body department. In fact, he might have been the best-looking man she'd ever seen in person. But what irked her was he just knew it. He flaunted it as if there was nothing else to him. Or maybe she was being down on him because she couldn't stand good-looking, rich men like her absent father, which wasn't really fair. In her eyes, hot, rich guys could always get anything they wanted, and it didn't matter who they might hurt in the process. Well, it was a good thing he didn't want her because he'd be in for a rude awakening.

She stood from the chair, his smirky lips still annoying the crap out of her. *God, this guy really thinks he's the shit.* If only she could stop looking at his lips, jaw, and broad shoulders. Maybe she shouldn't have stood yet.

"I'm not done, Scottine."

She sat. Did he have to say her name like that with that hot British accent of his? Was it British? She wasn't sure. She grumbled, "Sorry."

"Send a dozen red roses to Tamsin White. Her office address is in my contacts. The note shall say, 'Tamsin, please forgive me. I won't make the reservation tonight. Let's reconnect during the holidays when work slows down. All my best, Konrad.'"

Scottie wrote quickly, scoffing with each word. This was a kiss-off note, probably the nicest kiss-off she'd ever heard. After she'd written down the details, she looked back up at him, catching his amused gaze on her.

Maybe it was the sun that beamed rays through the floor-to-ceiling window, but he somehow managed to get even better-looking than before. How was that even possible? His crystalline blue eyes stared at her with an intensity that made her want to look away. She refused, feeling the need to relent in her stomach. He would not scare her. He would not bully her with his handsome ways.

"Ready for more?" His question was as insinuating as the other one.

"Umm … yes." Her throat went dry, to her dismay. *Damn.* She averted her gaze back to the safety of her notebook.

"Send a dozen white roses to Antonia Robuchon, to her home address, which is also in my contacts. The note shall say, 'Looking forward to dinner tonight.'"

Scottie's eyes snapped up to him. Anger bubbled inside her. How could she participate in this? His very blatant lies. Clearly, he was playing both of these women. Antonia apparently won the prize. Did she know what prize she won? Scottie pitied the women.

"Problem?" He didn't seem affected in the least.

Are you an idiot? Of course she had a problem. What woman wouldn't? Or ethical person, for that matter. But she'd have to pipe down. This was not her problem. Leaving this job because of her moral dilemma *would* be a problem for her. Rent wouldn't be paid. She'd have to suck it up.

Back to her notepad. "No problem."

"Make sure the flowers are delivered before the end of the day. Okay, Scottine?" He turned to face his computer before she could answer him.

What a pompous jerk. She stood up in relief and with an urgency to get out of his office. "Yes, sir."

He waved her off without so much as looking at

her, his attention on his computer screen.

"One more thing," Scottie said just before she reached the door. He looked up, surprise on his face by her brazen tone. "I go by Scottie, not Scottine."

His lips curled up to smirk at her again. "And I go by Konrad, not sir."

Her eyes zeroed in on his lips, which were parted and seductive like he kissed on a regular basis. She turned from him before her face betrayed her bold thought and escaped his office, her heart beating wildly.

By the time she got to her cube, seconds later, she was completely unsettled. Off balance. For her first job out of college, this was not what she expected. For some reason, she imagined her first job would be making coffee for some old guy. Collecting his mail and teaching him how to use the Internet. Maybe that was a bit unfair and dramatic—exactly how she'd been feeling lately. Truth was, Konrad might be too good-looking to work for. And when she'd been in his office, underneath the annoyance she'd felt toward him, she was intrigued.

Just focus on the work. Scottie had to remind herself and get Konrad and his smirking lips out of her mind. She did as she was told and found the women who would receive Konrad's flowers, all the while sighing at her part in his player's game. Because, clearly, he was a player.

She hated players with every fiber of her being. It made her think of her father. Her mother was indeed a cautionary tale that Scottie remembered every time she got close to a guy. That was why she never got close to a guy.

Scottie better just send the damn flowers and let it go.

Thirty minutes later, the flowers had been ordered. She glanced at the clock. Close to lunch. She was lucky she had some cash for a sandwich at the lunch kiosk she saw when she'd first entered the Korr Corp building. As she ran through her options, the sharp shriek of the phone startled her. Panicking, she stared at the phone. This being her first job, she'd never used a multi-line office phone before. It was terrifying. Like something out of the NASA command center.

She lifted the receiver, hoping the caller hadn't hung up. Stumbling over her words, she answered, "Mr. Korr's office. How may I help you?"

"It's Tamsin. Put me through to him." The voice was sharp and not in the playing mood. Scottie suspected the caller Tamsin and the Tamsin White she'd just sent flowers to were one and the same.

Scottie hesitated, glancing to his office across the aisle. She could see him through the glass wall typing on his keyboard. "Umm..."

"Are you daft? Patch me through." The British accent came through strong with her angry question.

"Let me see if he's available." Scottie pushed down hard on the hold button. *Calm down. Just calm down.* She could do this. She could figure out a telephone for God's sake. Taking in a breath, she scanned the other buttons, some labeled, some not, and set her flickering gaze on a button with Konrad's name printed on it. Relief came when she managed to call him on a second line without hanging up the first.

"What is it?" His clipped tone annoyed her. Had he no appreciation for screening angry women for him?

"Tamsin is on line one. Can I transfer her to you?" *Shit.* Scottie would have to figure out how to do that too.

He sighed heavily. "Ah, fuck."

His swear startled Scottie.

Konrad's inappropriateness continued, but his

swear was exasperated. Dread laced his voice. Scottie turned to face him through the glass wall, watching him rake his free hand through his dark golden hair. She felt sorry for him in a way, though he didn't deserve it. Tamsin, if she was indeed the same Tamsin White, had every right to call, ready to rip him a new one.

Finally, he said, "Tell her I'm on a call, and I'll get back to her when I can."

"She seems really upset…" Now Scottie felt sorry for Tamsin and actually wanted someone to rip Konrad a new one. He needed to be brought down a peg, of that Scottie was most certain.

"That's not my concern," he barked, meeting her gaze from across the aisle. "Do as I said, and tell her I'm on a call. Understand?"

Scottie looked back at the phone. She didn't want her face to betray her. Not on day one. She was suddenly hot in her black pants and long-sleeved, button-up shirt. *What a complete ass*. As far as Scottie was concerned, Tamsin losing out to Antonia was the best thing that could've happened to her. In an even tone, she said, "I understand."

"Fantastic, *Scottie*." The dial tone charged through the line with his dismissal.

Cursing under her breath, Scottie pushed on line one, bracing herself for another round of verbal melee. "I'm sorry. Mr. Korr is on a call at the moment. May I take a message and call-back number?"

"But of course he is." She grunted, drawing in a noisy sigh that hurt Scottie's ears. "You tell that tosser I've made a reservation for dinner at L'Atelier tonight at eight. He'd better be there."

Good luck with that.

Scottie wanted to tell her the truth. It pained her that she couldn't. "I will relay the message."

I'm a bad person.

Tamsin hung up with a swear and not a goodbye. Again, left with the dial tone raging in her ear, Scottie sighed, placing the receiver in the cradle. God, it was going to be a long day.

****

Almost five. Scottie counted down with her computer clock, relief coming every second. When five came, she finally relaxed. Every muscle in her body loosened. Working sucked. This was not what she expected. It had been almost four months since she'd graduated, and she expected to be in a real career, not desperate for a temp job because she'd run out of the money her grandmother had given her for college. Scottie kicked herself for not getting an internship in the spring as many of her fellow BBA classmates did. Scottie should not have dragged her feet to find a real job. Totally her own fault. She probably deserved a jerk boss for not getting her shit together sooner. Still, that seemed too cruel, considering how much of a jerk her boss had proven himself to be.

Scottie filled in her A-Plus Temporaries timesheet, writing in six hours of work. Six hours was better than no hours. The pay was decent, but she knew this would be temporary for sure. She'd need a permanent job. A career. She needed to take control of her adult life, now that her finances were her own problem and her struggling single mom wouldn't be able to offer any support. Scottie didn't want her to. Her mother had sacrificed enough for Scottie, her only child.

Scottie's gaze fell over Konrad Korr's name printed at the top of the timesheet. His signature authorized her paycheck. She'd have to remember that when he was being an ass and she wanted to tell him where to get off. But for some reason, she smiled when she thought about him, her body thrumming with light sensations. Her muscles tensed again with the realization of how much she was still curious about him despite his rollercoaster moods. *No, you can't think of him like that.* He was a womanizer and an arrogant ass. She should know better.

Standing from her desk, she pep-talked herself. Tomorrow would be better. She knew what to expect. She knew how to appease Konrad. Satisfied with the acceptance of her predicament, she stepped out of her cubicle. Konrad, moving around the corner, slammed into her at near full speed. She yelped, his large hands going for her, grabbing her under the armpits.

"*Verdammt*!" he said, his gaze wide. Never mind the awkward way he held her. "Are you all right? Did I knock the wind out of you?"

Scottie couldn't find a word. Language left her completely. Only the hot hands under her armpits, fingers too close to her nipples, had her full attention. To her dismay, waves of heat ran straight down where they shouldn't have been. She was turned on. No denying this blatant fact. *Oh God.*

Hot and humiliated, she wiggled free from him. "I'm fine. Did you have to come around that corner so fast?"

"You're right. I apologize for almost knocking you over." He stepped back, and stupidly she wanted his hands on her again.

Stop it.

The curve of his lips caught her attention. "I … uhh…" She stumbled over her words, still grappling with the way her body responded to him. Meeting his eyes again, she knew he'd caught her staring at his mouth. *Shit. What am I doing?* Taking her attention from him, she bent over to pick up her purse, which had fallen to the floor. "It's fine. No worries."

"Well, have a good night then. Sorry again."

"Thanks. You too." She slipped from under his magnetism and dashed out of the office. For the first time, she'd felt his male power. His sexual power. The power that made women gravitate to him. Despite how much she fought it, Scottie could understand it. She could totally understand why Tamsin was so pissed. If Scottie had met Konrad out in a bar, she might fall under his spell too.

She needed to get out of the Korr Corp building stat, and away from Konrad.

Thirty minutes later, Scottie eased her ten-year-old Nissan sedan into the driveway of the duplex house in the Heights she rented with Tara, her childhood friend.

Fresh-baked bread scented the small house. Tara was a chef, trying to get her catering business off the ground. She'd been an apprentice to a well-known chef who owned L'Atelier, the most upscale restaurant in Houston. Unfortunately, few of his patrons had called for her services once she'd struck out on her own. By the smell of the apartment and the bags and boxes all over the kitchen, Scottie concluded she'd finally gotten a gig.

"Tara," Scottie called, tossing her keys on the small dinette table. Tara stood from behind the island separating the kitchen from the dining area, a pissed-off look on her face. "Are you okay?"

Scottie grabbed a banana from the counter and peeled it.

"Those are my bananas," she snapped, stopping Scottie mid-bite.

Scottie lowered the banana. *What the hell is her problem?* "Thanks, Tara. I had a great first day at my new temp job. Thank you for asking."

Tara released a noisy breath. "It's the fourth of

the month, you know."

"Yeah…" Scottie knew what this was about.

Tara glowered at Scottie, her lips pursing, holding back terse words Scottie knew had been festering since September first. Scottie stalled. She wasn't in the mood for Tara's complaints. Not when she still felt her new boss's hands on her side-boobs.

The silence irked Scottie. She hated when Tara got that way. And, as usual, Scottie spoke first. "I get paid next Friday. You know I just started this job. Can you just spot me until then?" Scottie put the banana back on the counter. She wasn't hungry anymore.

"That's the fifteenth, Scottie. Rent is considered late on the tenth. You know that."

Scottie pushed her hair back. "So, you can't spot me until then?"

Tara's hand shot down, slamming against the counter, startling Scottie. "You still owe me a hundred dollars that I covered for you from last month's rent."

"Jesus, Tara. You know the money my grandmother left me ran out two months ago, and I just got this job after looking all summer for one."

Tara grunted. "Hardly."

Scottie's anger simmered. They'd had this hanging between them for months. "What is that supposed to mean?"

Tara shook her head. "You really didn't try, Scottie."

Crossing her arms over her chest, Scottie thought she might cry any moment. She hated fighting with Tara. "I'm sorry I couldn't find something suitable in *your* acceptable time frame."

"It's called being an adult, Scottie. You do what you have to do." Tara scrubbed her face. "Look, I can't cover for you this month. I'm barely making it, as you already know."

Scottie sighed. Tara was right. "What do you want me to do?"

Tara turned back to the cluttered counter. "I'm catering a last-minute dinner tonight, and I couldn't find affordable last-minute help. You can pay off the hundred by helping me tonight."

Hell no! Scottie groaned. Hospitality wasn't her game. With her luck, she'd trip and spill red wine on some rich woman's white couture dress. But did she really have another choice? "How long is it?"

Tara's eyes turned to slits. "It doesn't matter. You owe me."

She was right. Scottie did owe her. And she'd still owe her once the night was over. "Fine. I'll do it. But I'm not wearing an apron."

Tara tossed a folded apron at Scottie's head. "You *will* wear one. And you'll enjoy it."

Scottie sighed. There was no other choice.

Chapter Three

Konrad glanced at Pilar, the purr of his prized sports Mercedes coupe engine vibrating through him as he eased the car through the underground garage of the Museum District high-rise where Antonia lived. He caught Pilar uncross her long tan legs from the corner of his eye. Was he really about to take a woman into his inner circle? The circle he kept only for himself?

"You're not okay, are you?" She smoothed down her curtain of straight dark hair over her shoulder.

He parked the car, his gaze dancing over the tiny, fitted white dress barely covering the tops of her thighs. Thighs he knew like the back of his hand. "I just don't want to give you the wrong impression. That's all, love. You know I'm not the committing type."

She laughed, putting him at ease. Her black eyes twinkled in the dim garage light coming in through the windshield. "And I'm not either. I'm only twenty-one! So, don't worry. I know this doesn't mean anything."

Twenty-one. Seven years his junior. Sometimes he thought she could be older with her maturity. She was right though. It didn't mean anything. None of the women he dated meant anything. Not to be cruel, but it was a fact. All women he pursued knew this upfront. They all agreed, though some women later decided they couldn't be casual. Pilar hadn't been one of those women.

"Off we go, then." He rubbed her smooth thigh before he opened the door.

With his hand pressed against Pilar's lower back, Konrad knocked on the front door of Antonia's penthouse. Antonia's housekeeper Mary opened it, greeting them and offering to take Pilar's purse. Loud voices came from the living room where Konrad's friends had been talking and drinking, lounging on the art deco couches. Tylund was alone, which annoyed Konrad. Fabian swore everyone had a date. Melina, Antonia's best friend, was there sans a date as well.

"Good evening," Antonia said, standing from the couch and walking over to greet Konrad and Pilar.

As he always did, Konrad lifted her off the ground in a tight embrace and kissed her cheek. "My God, Antonia, how the hell did that tosser Fabian land a gorgeous woman like you?" The group laughed, agreeing with his sentiment.

"Shut up!" Fabian called from the bar, a champagne bottle overflowing in his hands.

She pressed against his shoulders in a silent demand to be released. He did so with as much grace as he had picked her up. "You're too kind." Antonia adjusted her conservative navy dress once her shoes touched the tiles.

"This is Pilar de los Santos, my *friend*."

A low chuckled rippled through the air. One of his asshole friends found the term amusing, not that those twats could offer any commentary on the subject. They'd both had their fair share of *friends*.

Antonia offered her hand to Pilar, who took it. "Hi, Pilar. Welcome. I'm Antonia. That's Fabian at the bar. And that's Melina." She pointed to everyone respectively who waved and greeted Pilar with kindness. "Tylund is the one on his phone."

One friend was missing from the introductions. Dallas hadn't arrived yet. If he also didn't have a date, there'd be hell to pay.

Pilar waved. "Hi, everyone."

"Take a seat, Pilly. I'll get you a glass of champagne," Konrad said, winking at her.

Antonia stopped him with a touch of her hand on his arm. "Thank you for the flowers, Konrad. They are beautiful."

He smiled at her, contemplating lifting her up again because he knew how much she hated it. Instead, he touched the tip of her nose in some weird, and very him, fashion. "You're welcome, love."

Konrad left the group to their own devices, hoping they wouldn't ask Pilar any questions. They knew the deal, though. He liked women. Dated lots of them. And he was private about it. *Just stop worrying.* It was no big deal. He had to remind himself. But by forcing himself to remain calm, he thought of Scottie again, and the awkward way he'd run into her. His palms still felt the weight of her. He tried to blink the memory away. *Why am I thinking of her?* On his approach of the bar, Konrad shoved Scottie to the back of his mind—though not too far back because she was still there.

Fabian gave him a curling grin and handed Konrad a heavy glass of scotch. "She's hot."

Konrad glanced at Pilar seamlessly chatting with the other women as if they all were best friends forever. Indeed, she was hot. Actually, she was perfect. Nice girl. Nice body. Nice lay. Good attitude. Low expectations. Perfect. "She's all right."

She was exactly what Konrad needed her to be.

Tylund came up behind them. "Leave it to this asshole to get a smoking-hot date on short notice." He punched Konrad on the shoulder. "It has to be the accent."

"It's my handsome face that gets me dates. And besides, it's not like you've ever come up short, mate." Konrad took a sip of his drink, thinking of Scottie again. She definitely wouldn't have a good attitude, but he suspected she had a nice body under her ill-fitting clothes.

"True." Tylund beamed. "I don't come up short in any way. I guarantee it." They cackled. Tylund once again bragged about his manhood, which he claimed was bigger than a baby's arm.

"This asshole…" Fabian pointed at Tylund, barely containing his laughter.

"So, where's *your* date, then?" Konrad asked, elbowing Fabian in the side.

"Well, you know, she had something come up last minute." Tylund waved his hands around, explaining, but it only made Konrad and Fabian laugh harder.

"I suppose Melina can be your date tonight. Poor girl," Konrad said.

"Yeah, right." Fabian chuckled, turning toward the bar. He poured three flutes of Krug. The bubbles foamed up nearly over the top, but only lingered at the rim. "Champagne for the ladies."

"I'll take them." Tylund took the glasses and walked to the living room, clearly desperate to get away from the bashing they gave him.

"That guy's a mess." Konrad shook his head, staring after him.

"I know." Fabian sipped his scotch. He was pensive, staring into the living room. "I can't imagine living like I was before Toni. You know, doing nothing meaningful. Blowing my trust fund. It was such a waste."

Konrad met his softened gaze. "That's a bit harsh, no?"

"It's true." He sighed, a far-off look in his eyes again. "I feel better now, like I'm doing something. Toni makes me want to be a better person."

Konrad sipped again. He could see his friend's transformation like night and day. Fabian had grown up so fast. Overnight practically. And for a woman. Konrad couldn't imagine that ever happening to him. He was too independent and focused. A woman would only resent him for putting his job first, and himself. He saw it firsthand with his own parents, felt the pain of it. As best as he could, Konrad pushed those thoughts down. He wanted to forget what happened with his parents. But in the midst of his reverie, noises from the kitchen took his attention. He glanced up from his drink only to meet eyes with the last person he'd thought he'd see.

Scottine Roberts. His temp.

What the fuck is Scottie doing here?

Fabian glanced back to the kitchen. "Oh, they're just the caterers."

Caterers? Why was Scottie catering? And of all the dinner parties she could possibly cater, what were the odds of her catering Konrad's friends' dinner party? It was like the universe conjured her up from his thoughts just to fuck with him.

Frozen, Konrad couldn't tear his eyes off Scottie. His heart raced, and the words didn't come. Scottie's lips parted, closing when another woman came up behind her with a tray. She turned to her, leaving Konrad abandoned from her stare. And he wanted her eyes again.

"Are you okay?" Fabian touched Konrad's arm, startling him.

"Uhh … yes, of course. I'm totally fine," Konrad rambled, grappling with what to do next. Should he tell Fabian about Scottie? For the first time, he had no idea what to do in regards to a woman.

"Care for a salmon puff?" Scottie's voice slipped in the silence between Konrad and Fabian.

Konrad waited for a greeting from her. Like, "Hey, Konrad." Or "Fancy meeting you here, boss." Or some other indication that she knew him. Nothing. She'd remained steady with her silver tray held out to them.

He didn't know if he should call her out. No one had ever done that to him. In fact, women bent over backward to know him. An unprecedented stream of exhilaration rushed through his body. What was she trying to prove?

Fabian reached for a salmon puff, awkwardly proclaiming, "They look great." He popped the salmon puff in his mouth. "The Decadent Chick Catering owner was the apprentice to the L'Atelier executive chef. Isn't that right?"

Great. It seemed Fabian sensed the weirdness.

Scottie's hazel eyes gripped Konrad's while she should have been looking at Fabian. "Yes, that's right. Would you like to try?"

Konrad couldn't move, couldn't respond. *Say something. Do something, dammit!*

"Have one, Konrad," Fabian urged, taking another. After swallowing, he said to Konrad, "This is Scottie. She's assisting Tara, the chef and owner, tonight. This big German is Konrad Korr."

Her full pink lips curled up in a languid way, making him remember touching her only hours ago. "It's nice to meet you, *sir.*"

Her words stunned him. Sir? She called him sir? Clearly, she was toying with him.

Konrad eased back into his smooth ways, nodding at her with a challenging smirk on his own lips. "You as well, *Scottie.*" He nearly said Scottine.

The awkward silence stretched between them. Konrad took a salmon puff of his own and opened his mouth, aware he had Scottie's full attention. Something had changed between them. He couldn't help feel the heat of their exchange and the desire he felt in his loins to be close to her again.

Pilar and Melina came up behind them, jolting Konrad to remember there were other people in the penthouse, not just Scottie and her amazing eyes making him question himself. He straightened, turning his attention to the women, though still thinking about Scottie.

Polite and proper, Pilar plucked a salmon from the tray. "Looks very good."

Scottie gifted her a tight smile, and Konrad knew that was meant for him.

Konrad set his gaze on Scottie, wondering if she would crack under her blatant lie of not knowing him. And why the hell did he care about it so much? When Marisol returned, Scottie would be history. Forgotten. Just another woman he'd interacted with.

The longer he stared at her, the more he knew that couldn't be true.

"Aren't they good, Kon?" Pilar snaked her arm around Konrad's waist, lifting a puff to his lips with her other hand.

He reluctantly opened his mouth, feeling ashamed, not that he had any reason to. He was completely aware everyone looked at him. Pilar purred, running her hand down to his hip bone. All eyes on that motion, too. But only Scottie's disapproving gaze gave him pause. When Pilar and Melina walked back to the couch a second later, Scottie's remained, her eyebrows raised. The same way she'd raised it when he'd asked her to send flowers to two different women.

This looks bad. Even he could acknowledge that.

"Looks like Toni needs more champagne." Fabian grabbed the bottle off the bar and left Konrad alone with Scottie.

Not even a second passed before Scottie said, "You're the last person I thought I'd run into."

"'*It's nice to meet you, sir?*' Are you serious?" He put his scotch glass down.

Scottie glanced at his friends in the living area. "I just thought it would be easier that way."

"Why?" He supposed he understood her logic. She might be embarrassed. And God knew how much his friends would rag on him later.

"I don't know … it just is. No need for explanations." Her gaze lowered to the few remaining puffs. The crew certainly had a voracious appetite. "Besides, I want to be anonymous to your girlfriends."

Her sarcasm irked him, but her boldness excited him in a way he wasn't used to. Women were never this hard to get on with. She made it practically impossible.

"And by that you mean…" He waited, refusing to let her look away from him.

She shrugged, shifting her gaze to the living room again, which annoyed him. "I don't want to get attacked on your behalf."

"That's absurd." Did she really believe that? Damn her judgement of him.

The freckles on the bridge of her nose popped more in the lighting. He'd been so close to her he could count them if he wanted. He dropped his gaze to the rest of her. Black skirt, inches above her knees, displaying smooth tan legs. Nice body confirmed.

And that apron. *God, stop it!*

Scottie narrowed her eyes at him as if she knew what he was thinking.

"I saw that." Apparently, she did know.

"What?" He feigned innocence.

"You looked at my legs." Her voice was tight.

"I noticed them, Scottine. There is a difference." No, he *looked*. Actually, he gawked. And he should not.

"It's Scottie."

The challenge between them sizzled like a live wire. This was not his office, and they were acting accordingly. Tomorrow, however, they would be in his office. Then what?

Tara called Scottie from the kitchen. She turned, dread on her face. "Have another." She shoved the last two puffs in his mouth and spun on her heels back to the kitchen.

He watched her ass moving underneath her skirt, mind reeling, as he chewed the hors d'oeuvre seasoned with her fingers. He chewed faster, his body alive with sensations he wished would go away. But he could not take his eyes off her ass. Without a look back to him, she turned the corner and was gone from sight. His heart thumped. This woman. He had no idea what to do with her.

"Konrad!" Antonia called from the living room where everyone had gathered, even Dallas, who stood next to a gorgeous brunette in fitted jeans and a nude-tone crop top.

Konrad had been too submerged in his thoughts—and his very real, very surprising attraction to Scottie—to answer.

Fabian waved him over. "Come here and bring your drink."

Shit. What was this? An intervention? No way. There was nothing to intervene on. With reluctance, he strode to the living area and sat next to Pilar, who rubbed his thigh casually. He imagined it was Scottie's hand. *For God's sake.*

"What's this about?" Konrad asked. He had his own issue to contend with.

"I have no clue," Tylund chimed in, turning to Melina, who shrugged.

"Fucking say something." Dallas's East Texas

accent came out strong. His date giggled, cuddling against his side. She seemed a bit young for his normal taste.

Fabian and Antonia gazed at each other like lovesick puppies, their fingers intertwined, their smiles growing wider as if they shared some secret. Konrad grew conflicted. Something deep inside him knew what the couple had to say.

Antonia started after she and Fabian finished eye-screwing each other. "Well, we have some good news. First, I'd like to announce that my mom is actually doing better despite all signs and prognosis. So, we are celebrating that."

Everyone cheered. Konrad lifted his glass. He'd known what it was like to lose a mother. His whole heart went out to Antonia. He drank, as did everyone else.

Fabian nodded to his left, summoning Scottie to pass out champagne flutes. He pointed at the group.

Scottie refused to look at Konrad as she handed him a glass of champagne. In a low voice, he said, "Thank you, Scottie."

She nodded under reddened cheeks. Still no eye contact.

"First, everyone please get a champagne flute. We have another announcement," Fabian said.

Konrad's instinct was right. He knew exactly what they were going to announce. He held the flute stem between his fingers. Dallas, who sat next to Konrad, elbowed his side. He knew too.

When every person held a champagne flute, Fabian began. "This has been such a whirlwind, meeting Antonia again after so many years and then chasing her down until she wanted to be with me."

Everyone laughed. Antonia smiled, her dark eyes glistening.

Fabian continued, "I don't know how I got so fucking lucky with this one, but fuck, she is the best thing that has ever happened to me. She makes me want to be a better person."

Konrad couldn't look at him anymore. This was too much. He'd felt too many new emotions, uncomfortable emotions. A longing grew inside him, making him feel lonely and lost a little bit.

"And I think I offer her some things too. Maybe?" Fabian laughed.

Konrad heard the pop of their kiss, and he knew it was wrong to not face his friends when they were about to change their lives forever in his presence.

"Last night when I picked Toni up from yoga class, I couldn't hold back. I couldn't wait. Because when I looked over at her, all sweaty and in spandex, I knew I couldn't go another day without her being with me. Permanently. So, I asked her to marry me, and she said yes."

Konrad took in the sight, his throat aching. He averted his gaze and caught Scottie staring at him from across the living room, the tray pressed against her chest. Her eyes were soft, her mouth in a slight curve. He gasped, getting Pilar's attention, who in turn rubbed his leg again. Scottie turned away, walking back down the hall to the kitchen.

"We know it's so fast, but when you know, you know, right?" Antonia said, taking Konrad's attention from Scottie. She'd held up her ring finger, showing off a gigantic diamond ring.

When you know, you know... Konrad had heard that saying ad nauseam. It didn't make sense to him. It couldn't...

The women swooned at the ring. The men stood and congratulated Fabian one by one.

"Congratulations, mate." Konrad and Fabian embraced and patted each other on the back. "You honestly couldn't have done better. She could have, but you already knew that."

Fabian grinned. "Fuck you!" He grew serious. "She's everything to me, Konrad. Seriously, I can't imagine being without her."

I can't imagine being without her. Fabian's words gave him pause. Konrad had lived his life so he wouldn't have to find out what that meant, with great success.

"That sounds awful, mate."

"You'll eat those words when it happens to you." Fabian winked at him, turning his attention to Dallas.

Konrad glanced back to the bar where Scottie had stood. He wondered if he ever would eat his words.

Chapter Four

Dressed in beige pants and another white button-up shirt, Scottie walked through the small hallway connecting the bedrooms to the living room. She was still reeling about the night before, her confrontation with Konrad on her mind. But the part that perplexed her the most was his reaction to his friend's engagement. He seemed sad. Lost too, maybe. Maybe he was capable of other emotions besides chauvinism and arrogance.

"It's September fifth, Scottie." Tara's voice ripped Scottie from her thoughts.

And? Didn't they just have a conversation about this? "Yes, it is." Scottie grabbed her purse off the couch, checking her cell phone for messages, of which there were none.

Tara sucked air through her teeth. She was in another mood. "You need to give me your share of the rent."

Scottie squeezed her eyes shut, a headache looming. Had she not listened? "I told you I don't get paid until Friday the fifteenth, Tara. We already discussed this."

Tara lifted her hand in frustration. "I never said I would spot you for this month too." She lowered her hand, glowering at Scottie as if they hadn't been friends since they were three years old. "If you can't pay by the ninth, there will be some changes around here."

Taken completely off guard, Scottie stepped back. Her breath hitched in her throat. Tara had never threatened her that way. Never had made her feel like she was the worst person in the world. "Jesus, Tara..."

Scottie couldn't finish though, because Tara's boyfriend, Brett, traipsed into the living room, wearing only a towel slung low around his waist. *Her* towel.

"Hey, loser," Brett said, ruffling Scottie's hair as he passed.

"Get off me!" Scottie smoothed down her hair, furious and hurt that her best friend would be so heartless.

Brett kissed Tara on the forehead and took the banana Scottie had her eye on from the counter. With a lump in her throat, Scottie turned. She needed to leave.

"I'm not kidding, Scottie," Tara barked with her finger pointing at Scottie accusingly. The conversation was over.

Brett groped Tara, kissing her like he'd never see her again.

Scottie groaned at the display. Tara could have done much better than Brett. Scottie grabbed her keys on the way out the front door.

On time, Scottie walked on her worn pumps through the lobby of Korr Properties, waving at Susan, who'd answered a call just as she walked in.

Butterflies fluttered violently in her stomach on the walk to her desk. Konrad had arrived. She could smell his fresh cologne as she advanced in the suite. She was anxious. She was excited, though she didn't want to admit it to herself. Would he bring up the dinner party? Would she? What would he say?

With all the thoughts rolling in her head, she couldn't prepare herself for what she saw. A beautiful woman, refined and blatantly wealthy, eased out of his office in a cream dress holding a Prada purse in her delicate hand. She was tall with dark hair, perfectly coifed, understated makeup to show off her sculptured features. God, she was gorgeous. Scottie froze, her stomach dropping a little. This woman looked like someone Konrad would date.

She leaned in to kiss his cheek. A seductive curl on his lips made Scottie think she'd judged him correctly the first time. He was a player. He liked women. Tamsin. Pilar. This woman. Who else? Yes, Scottie had pegged him correctly.

"It's so nice to see you, Konrad," she said, her voice melodic and soothing. She ran her finger over his jaw in a dignified, yet intimate, caress. They *knew* each other. No doubt about it. "Sorry I came by on a whim. I look forward to seeing you tonight."

Yes, they certainly knew each other.

"Thanks for coming by, Anisette. You're looking gorgeous as always, love." He winked. Did this man know no boundaries? He'd seen Scottie and knew he had an audience.

Beautiful Anisette turned on her Louboutins and eased down the corridor, the red soles flashing at Scottie. Mocking her. Telling her she could never have a man like Konrad. *Wait. What?* Scottie perished that thought quickly because she didn't want Konrad. No way.

Scottie's gaze moved up Konrad's body. His fancy shoes, his tailored pants, his fitted jacket, his shoulders, his bright-blue eyes staring at her. Attractive was an understatement. He was beyond that. It was almost cruel to be that good-looking. If she was honest, she'd have to admit he was the kind of man who was easy to fall for.

That didn't always fare well for people, her mother included. Scottie wiped the stars out of her eyes because reality demanded it and she hardened herself to his charms.

"Good morning, Scottie," he said, pulling her from her digression. "After you get settled, come in my office. I have a task for you."

"Okay." Walking as fast as she could to her cube,

she threw down her purse. And just before she grabbed her notepad, she glanced at herself in the reflection of her cell phone screen, taking inventory of herself. Sighing, she put the phone down on the desk and went to Konrad's office.

"Close the door," Konrad said upon her arrival.

She closed it and waited for more, all the while maintaining her wild heartbeat.

He leaned back in his chair, arm up over the headrest. "I need you to send some contracts over to legal for some Korr Properties."

So, he's not going to mention the dinner party. Okay, she could deal with that. Probably was better that way. Nodding, she sat in the same chair she'd sat in the day before and prepared for his direction.

She looked up, the silence growing thick in the office. He gazed at her, considering her in a way that made her self-conscious. For a moment, she thought he would bring up the dinner party, because he looked at her the same way he'd looked at her then. But he didn't. It was business as usual. Exactly what she should expect.

"I'm taking you down to Korr Solutions."

"I thought you said I'm only doing work for Korr Properties?" She was too breathless.

"Correct." He nodded. "It's just a tour."

"Sure. Okay. That sounds good." *Please stop looking at me that way.* The power of attractiveness had never been so in her face before.

A notification chimed on his cell phone. With his attention on the screen, he said, "Also, I need you to call Christine, my personal shopper, who is in my contacts. Tell her I need a gift, preferably Chanel, for a woman. And make sure it's sent to Anisette Bonnenfont today. In addition, add a personal note saying, 'Raincheck for tonight? Something has come up. My best, Konrad.'"

"My God, how many women are there?" Scottie didn't look up from her notepad. The thump of his cell phone on his desk let her know she'd gone too far.

Their eyes met once again.

"Do you have something to say, Scottine?" His voice was surprisingly calm, though he shouldn't be. He was the boss, after all, and clearly she crossed a line.

But his lips curled up in humor. Was he making fun of her? The notion made her hot with anger. Was she a joke to him just like the rest of his women?

Scottie clenched her jaw, and a slow head shake followed. "I don't have anything to say."

"Are you sure? Because you seemed to have a lot to say seconds ago." He placed his thick forearms against his desk, his palms facing down. "You know, Scottie, if you can't do the job, you should let me know now. I can find a replacement in no time."

Resistance tensed every muscle in her body. She needed this job. She needed him. "I can certainly do this job, Konrad."

His intensity made her self-conscious. Naked even. Damn him. Her whole body throbbed under his stare. And as ridiculous as it was, she imagined what it might be like to be naked under him.

"Is there anything else you need me to do?" Scottie's mouth dried out. She was desperate to leave, to be away from him and his pull on her.

"Yes." He looked at his computer screen. "I need you to set up a meeting with Bayou Sling Brewery."

Scottie wrote fast, still hyperfocused on the blood surging through her veins. "Any specific date and time this week?"

"Later this week. They aren't a priority." Another chime from his cell phone took his attention.

"So why meet with them?" *Just shut up and take*

notes, Scottie. The question was for herself, not him. This temp thing was not going well.

Amusement colored his face. "They don't have enough investors." His eyebrows furrowed. Scottie was done talking. "I'm not in this business to give property away, Scottie. It's always about the bottom line. You should have learned that in college. Now you can leave."

Scottie was conflicted. He was clearly a man who only satisfied his own pleasure. Did he ever consider anyone else? He seemed annoyed.

Just like that, she detached from the magnetic pull he had on her and stood. Three months of taking orders from Konrad seemed like a long time. And with that twirling in her head, she straightened and marched out of his office.

Once she was in her cube, she dialed the number to his personal shopper. The phone rang, giving Scottie a focal point. She needed to get her mind off Konrad.

On the fourth ring, a nasally voice answered. "Personal shopper services."

"Uh … hi…" Scottie didn't know how to begin. She'd never called a personal shopper services line before.

"Hello?" the nasally voice asked.

"Hi, yes. I'm calling on behalf of Konrad Korr."

"Ah, yes, Mr. Korr. Are you an employee?"

"Yes … err … no. I'm his temporary assistant."

"I suppose Marisol had her baby?"

How often did Konrad use personal shopper services? "Yes, she did. I'm filling in for three months."

"Please let Mr. Korr know his surprise nursery set to Marisol was sent out and should be delivered in the morning."

"Nursey set?"

"Yes. He bought her the whole catalog,

practically." She laughed. "He's so generous."

That wasn't expected. Scottie paused. Konrad had bought his assistant a whole nursery set? And he was generous?

"I'll tell him." Each word was practically its own sentence.

"And you are?"

"I'm Scottie Roberts."

"Hello, Scottie. I'm Christine. I handle Mr. Korr's account." She paused again. "How can I help you?"

Scottie was still stuck on the new information about Konrad. He also bought gifts for employees, not just the women in his life? Or was Marisol a woman in his life? *Oh God…* She'd have to stop her train of thought.

"Yes. Of course. Mr. Korr would like to send a gift to a…" Scottie scrolled through the contacts in his email program. "… Ms. Anisette Bonnenfont."

"Ahh, yes, Anisette." Christine chuckled. "Let me guess, something Chanel?"

"Right, something Chanel." Scottie bit down hard to keep a snarky comment from coming forth. Only the wealthy knew this kind of privilege. Like Scottie's father, the man she never really knew.

"I have the perfect item. Let me email you a picture of this gorgeous watercolor print scarf. Are you using Marisol's email?"

"No. You can send it to korrtemp@KorrCorp.biz."

"Fantastic. Give me just one second."

The email popped up immediately, and the scarf was absolutely gorgeous. Screen-printed watercolor flowers on silk. And over four hundred dollars. *Shit.* Four hundred dollars might get Tara off Scottie's back. At least for a day.

"It's perfect." What else could Scottie say? If she was Anisette, she would cherish that Chanel scarf, but she imagined Anisette probably had a collection of Chanel scarves.

"Wonderful!" Christine's enthusiasm made Scottie smile, even though inside she was still perplexed.

"Mr. Korr would like the scarf delivered as soon as possible. Can you deliver it by lunchtime?"

"Not a problem. I'll see to it myself."

Scottie heard clicking on a computer keyboard.

"Is there anything else I can help you with?"

"No. That will be all." Her mind swam.

"Thank you for calling personal shopper services. If I can assist you in any other way, please let me know. Goodbye, Scottie."

The dial tone buzzed in Scottie's ears, and she only had one question. Who the hell was Konrad Korr?

Chapter Five

Konrad met Dallas at Halman Hotel for lunch. The two men had been discussing a joint venture, an upscale boutique hotel. Konrad hadn't embarked on that territory yet, and it had been a dream of his. As heir of the Halman Hotel chain, Dallas was the best man to go into business with.

At the Mariposa bar attached to the Halman Hotel in the heart of the Museum District, Konrad drank a short glass of scotch, neat. With the way Scottie made him feel, he needed a drink to get himself straightened out. What was it about her that ruffled him so much? Besides the obvious, which was that she was stunning. He'd been with stunning women on most days of the week though. She was something else he couldn't pinpoint.

"Hey, man." Dallas came up behind him, tapping him on the shoulder, startling him. "Sorry I'm late. Was crunching some numbers upstairs."

"As a JVP of Finance does." Konrad shook Dallas's hand. In all sincerity, Dallas was the one friend he trusted most. Though rough around the edges, considering he spent the majority of his childhood on a cattle ranch in East Texas, Dallas had a lot in common with Konrad. They both were dedicated to their work and to expanding their empires.

Dallas sat, nodding at the cute bartender who apparently knew exactly what he wanted. In seconds, she placed a Jack and Coke in front of him. He winked in appreciation. Not two seconds passed before he'd taken a hefty gulp, nearly emptying the glass. Looked like he'd needed a drink too.

Dallas knocked on the wooden bar with a heavy knuckle after he'd set his glass down. "I sure as hell needed that. So, what's going on?"

"What did you think about Fabian's dinner party last night?" Konrad surprised himself with his question.

Dallas shook his head. "Antonia has that son of a bitch by the balls." He took another drink, the last of it. He chuckled, maybe feeling the same disbelief Konrad felt. "Lucky bastard."

Perhaps not.

"I must admit, he does look ridiculously happy." Konrad recalled the look on Fabian's face when he'd announced his engagement to Antonia. He looked absolutely smitten. Antonia was his world, and there was no question about it.

"She is a lovely woman," Konrad added. Antonia was more than that. Had to be. Fabian had been more of a ladies' man than Konrad. In fact, Konrad assumed he and Fabian would be bachelors for life. If Antonia could make him fall... Well, that meant it *was* possible to fall, which was a disconcerting thought.

"Fabian better not fuck it up is all I'm saying."

Konrad looked Dallas square in the eyes. "Could you allow yourself to fall like that?"

Dallas didn't answer straightaway. He mulled over the question, looking in his empty glass like a psychic looks at a crystal ball. "Let's just say I did fall for someone, but out of my own stupidity, I lost her. Seems like a lifetime ago now."

Konrad was shocked. He'd never heard Dallas mention this before. From that revelation, Konrad concluded that falling in love appeared to be either the best thing or the worst thing that could happen to a person. "Well, mate, we don't have to worry about running out of women. We'll always attract them. Even when we're fat, disgusting bastards."

Dallas grunted. "How do you figure?"

"We have accents. Women love accents."

"Mine is nothing exotic like yours."

Konrad laughed. "If only they knew who I really am, they'd stay far away from me."

"Oh, come on. You're being hard on yourself." Dallas punched his friend in the shoulder.

Perhaps. Emotions rose up in him again as he thought of everything that had happened the last couple of days. A change of subject would fare him well. "Where the hell is the lunch menu? What kind of two-bit operation are you running here, Halman?"

Dallas punched Konrad again, that time not as light. He waved over the bartender. "Bea, what do you recommend for lunch?"

"Filet mignon and sautéed spinach?" Bea set her slim hand on the bar. Konrad noticed the shiny cherry-red varnish on her petite nail beds. She was coquettish indeed, and she might be Konrad's one-night-stand type if she didn't work for one of his best friends. Which brought him to another thing. Scottie…

"Works for me," said Dallas, answering Bea. "You good with that, Kon?"

Konrad nodded.

With a thumbs-up, Dallas turned to Bea. "Two."

Once Bea had left to fulfill their orders, Konrad took a sip of his drink, nearly draining it, his thoughts on Scottie again and the secret they shared. He still didn't understand why she'd opted out of acknowledging him as her boss. And why it bothered him so deeply.

Dallas nudged Konrad. "What's wrong, man? I can see the wheels turning in your head."

"I'm a bit out of sorts today." Konrad glanced out past the bar to the fountain off Main Street, the crystalline water streams gleaming in the sun.

"Is it about business? Don't worry about those

hotel locations. My guys are researching. I got that handled. I'll have some lots to show you by next week."

He shook his head. "No... I'm confident about that, mate." Konrad knew if he told Dallas about Scottie, he'd have to admit some feelings to himself, which seemed small compared to the unburdening of it. "It's the oddest thing..."

"What is?"

Konrad drew in a breath. "You remember that girl from last night? The server?"

"Dark-haired girl? Brown eyes?"

"I think they're hazel." Not think, knew. He knew they were hazel. Gold and olive, her irises were completely mesmerizing.

Dallas's eyebrows lifted. "Yeah, I remember her. Why?"

"She's my temporary assistant while Marisol is out on maternity leave." Konrad wanted to be casual and factual about who she was, but his voice betrayed him. He was bothered.

Dallas's eyes grew wide. "She's what?"

"Crazy, right?" Immediately, he regretted his decision to tell Dallas. In three months, Scottie would be a non-issue.

"That's more than crazy." Dallas pressed on, though Konrad waved off the conversation. He was done with it. Dallas was not. "You didn't mention it."

"No." Konrad quickly became aware at the absurdity of the conversation and his feelings.

You looked at my legs. Konrad conjured up that moment between them, a smile threatening on his face. He was so inappropriate, but he wanted to look at her legs, her toned, seductive legs. Had Scottie any idea how seductive she was? He guessed not, since she'd worn another bland outfit that morning.

"And she didn't mention it, either…"

Konrad looked back at his friend. "No, she did not."

"And why?" Dallas wasn't going to let up.

"She thought it would be better to not acknowledge each other." Konrad dropped his gaze to his glass again. He couldn't look Dallas in the eyes with a lie on his lips. "It's fine. It's not a big deal or anything."

"Except it is a big deal. I've known you for a while. Since Harvard. You wouldn't mention it if it wasn't. Right?" Dallas waited for an answer Konrad didn't want to admit to. He knew him so well. And because Dallas knew him so well, a grin parted his lips after a realization on his part. "Wait … no fucking way!"

"What?" Game over. Konrad tugged on his tie, feeling choked by his own silent admission. He must be losing his edge. He slapped the bar. "Who do I need to shag to get another drink around here?"

Dallas grinned. "You can't get out of his conversation, Kon. Do you like that waitress?"

Konrad gave his friend a direct look. "No, mate. I don't fucking fancy her! She's not even my type."

Dallas furrowed his brow. "You mean because she has two jobs and not a trust fund?"

Konrad was full of shit, and Dallas was absolutely right. Konrad's rotation of women lived his wealthy lifestyle. They required it. Furthermore, he understood them, what they needed. A Chanel purse for a broken date. A Cartier bracelet for a broken promise. They always knew how to settle down when he'd offered a gift. Konrad sensed Scottie was not like that. There was something too innocent about her. He suspected she'd require more than a Cartier bracelet for a broken promise.

"Oh, wait a goddamn minute." Dallas pushed

Konrad's arm, nearly knocking it off the bar. That would be the grand revelation, then. "I see what's going on here."

"Hey! Watch the bespoke shirt." Konrad had officially lost his fight. The thing he wanted to keep to himself, Dallas was about to announce to the world.

"You're bent out of shape because she didn't acknowledge you. And how could any woman not acknowledge *you*!" Dallas howled. His perception was immaculate. If only he'd use that keen sense in business only and not in deciphering Konrad's innermost secrets.

"For God's sake," Konrad muttered, quite mad at himself. With women like Pilar and Anisette ready for his bed at the drop of a hat, he should be focusing on them and not his attraction to his temp, who clearly was not impressed with him in the least.

But it was true, though. Every bloody thing Dallas said.

"Finally, a woman who hasn't fallen for your charms in two seconds of knowing you." Dallas was having too good a time with the information.

Konrad grew serious, evening out his emotions. "I'm her boss, so she's just being professional, I'm sure. I commend it. Besides, have you not seen Pilar?"

"Oh, I have seen Pilar, my friend. But that's not the point, now is it?" Dallas was serious too.

God. He was right again.

Bea arrived with perfect timing. Konrad couldn't be more grateful to her. She placed their plates on the bar. "Two filet mignons for our handsomest patrons."

"You have to say that because you work for me."

"Uh-uh, Halman. You're just a junior VP. She doesn't work for you just yet." Konrad winked at a giggling Bea. Konrad needed to get at least one jab in. He'd lost the whole damn fight.

****

Back at the office, Konrad felt a bit more at ease, even when he received a thank-you email from Antonia for attending the engagement party. Konrad responded with the enthusiasm he knew his friends deserved. However, it all left him with the same longing he'd felt at the engagement dinner. He'd hoped that nagging feeling would subside sooner rather than later.

Konrad passed Susan at reception, waving as he walked through the doors leading into the Korr Properties suite. A few employees stopped him for signatures on documents as he walked to his office. The time had come to take Scottie on the grand tour of Korr Solutions. Excitement made his feet move faster to his office.

As he turned the corner, he heard Scottie's voice, even as low as it was. He paused, coming to a complete stop at the edge of her cube. Her words became clearer. She was on the phone.

"What do you mean I don't qualify for a credit line? I have never had a credit card before." Silence passed for several beats, and when she spoke again, she was indignant. "This makes no sense at all. How can you deny me when I don't have any delinquencies as a negative mark against me? No, I can't get a co-signer."

His heart clenched. Was she in trouble? Did she have financial problems?

"Look, I just need a credit card with a thousand-dollar credit limit. I have been banking with you since I was eighteen. That's five years! Isn't that worth something?" The distress overflowed from her voice.

Konrad was compelled to act in some way but didn't know how or what.

She must have heard him move, and at the moment she faced him, her face turned red, likely from her embarrassment, even though she had nothing to be embarrassed about. This touched him in a way he'd not anticipated.

Her mouth parted the moment their eyes met. She was completely frozen. The voice on the other end of the line sounded from the receiver, though she didn't respond right away. Scottie closed her mouth. Konrad felt bad that he'd caught her. She looked mortified.

Calmer, she said into the receiver, "I understand. I will have to get back to you. Goodbye." She hung up the phone. "Mr. Korr?"

Konrad lifted his eyebrow. "Miss Roberts?"

Her cheeks blushed. "Uh... Is there something I can help you with?"

The grand tour of Korr Solutions seemed so trivial after what he'd just heard, but she was his temp, and he could only be concerned about that. It was hard to forget the desperation in her voice, though. The mortification on her face. "Can you be ready in five minutes?"

"Yes, of course. Is there something wrong?" Her eyes widened, and she looked so innocent, like she'd never had a deviant thought in her life.

"I want to take you down to Korr Solutions for the tour." Konrad's voice was softer than he expected.

"Yes, of course," she said, stumbling over her words. "I'll go to your office in five minutes."

He nodded and walked across the aisle into his office. He was more perplexed than he ever had been. Dallas was right. Scottie didn't swoon for him upon meeting him. Didn't even give him any indication that she thought he was a decent guy. And though they'd only known each other a day, Konrad was drawn in. He was intrigued. For the first time, he thought, as disconcerting and unprecedented as it was, he could easily swoon for her.

Chapter Six

Scottie walked to the ladies' room as fast as she could. Humiliation was too soft a word to describe how she felt. Konrad overhearing her conversation was mortifying to say the least.

He wouldn't understand. She doubted he'd ever had financial problems in his life. Where would she turn? She refused to track down her father, wherever he was. He'd been nonexistent to her. No, she needed to do this on her own. No banks. No begging for handouts. She'd have to make some serious decisions. She was an adult and needed to stand on her own two feet. Not that she'd ever had anyone else to stand on.

When she returned to her cube, Konrad was waiting for her outside of his office. He'd been talking to another employee, whom Scottie didn't know, pointing at a piece of paper. On her approach, his eyes met hers, and there was something softer in them. Something that oddly soothed her.

"There she is," he said, sending tingles down Scottie's legs with his surprising words. He directed to the older women, "Let's pick this up later."

The woman nodded, retrieving the document and pivoting in the opposite direction.

Is he going to say something about my personal call?

"Off we go." He walked down the hall, with Scottie on his heels.

In the elevator, Scottie stood across the small vestibule from Konrad. When their eyes met, she smiled nervously, looking away. Hyperaware of herself, she could count her heartbeats. *One. Two. Three.* Dear God, the two-floor descent shouldn't have lasted that long.

He smelled so good, though. Like fresh laundry. And a spice she couldn't identify. Or bergamot, maybe? His whole house probably smelled like that. His sheets … his towels… And why was she thinking about his towels?

"What's on your mind, Scottine?"

His electric words moved her, soaring through her flesh. She could feel each syllable in her stomach, and it spiraled in response. The conversation she'd had with the bank was worlds away.

She shook her head. "Nothing."

He chucked low, but it sounded as if his mouth were only inches from her ear. "Don't be nervous. The Solutions crew is much more fun than me." She looked up in time to catch him wink at her. His blue eyes glistened in the fluorescent lighting that normally made everything look hideous. He was far from hideous.

"That can't be easy to accomplish."

His laugh was deep and succulent. "Cheeky."

Just then, the elevator opened. *Thank God*. Being in such close proximity to Konrad was dangerous. It was both disconcerting and exhilarating—exactly what she'd felt about him thus far.

Glass doors with *Korr Solutions* spelled out in wide chrome letters faced them. It was modern, not traditional with dark woods and brass grommets on distressed leather seating like Korr Properties. Both suites were gorgeously decorated. Konrad spared no expense.

He pulled open the door with the chrome handle. "After you."

His scent enveloped her as she slipped by him to enter the suite. Inside, the reception area was done in white with dark slate-gray carpet and white modern leather chairs with chrome frames. Black and white abstract art prints lined the walls.

"This is really nice." Scottie marveled, only to be caught off balance when Konrad's fingers pressed against her back. She jumped, and his hand fell away.

"This way." He pointed past the long white marble reception desk. As they approached, he greeted the attractive blonde donning a headset. "Sandy, love. How are things?"

Scottie was sure he shouldn't be calling his employees "love." This guy was an HR nightmare. Sandy seemed to like it, though. She blushed, her dark eyes sparkling like polished onyx stones. Who wouldn't like it, though? A pang of unwelcome jealousy shot through her. God, she needed to stop her ridiculousness.

"Fantastic!" Sandy answered—too brightly in Scottie's opinion.

"This is Scottie, the temporary Marisol." He glanced back to Scottie, grinning.

Scottie frowned. What woman wasn't temporary to him? "Hi."

Sandy waved. "Nice to meet you."

"All right then, let's get to it." He opened the doors leading into the suite, and Scottie passed through.

Inside, the suite was exactly like the reception: sleek, slate-gray, white tiles, abstract line art along the walls. Scottie liked the private cubes, considering what happened earlier with her interrupted private call. She needed privacy around him.

"Down this hall are the servers for our KCloud service for data storage." He pointed to double doors with a sign: *IT Only*. Just as they turned the corner, a man, a cute-ish man, nearly crashed into them with his sharp turn.

Konrad gave him a playful whack on the shoulder. "Jeff, you sneaky bastard!"

Jeff laughed nervously, Scottie noted. His brown gaze shifted to Scottie for a moment, a half smile on his lips. "Konrad! I didn't know you were coming down here."

"I need to keep you lazy asses on your toes." Konrad grinned.

Jeff rubbed his shoulder, grunting. He turned his eyes to Scottie, an obvious appreciation in the way he looked at her. "Who did you bring with you?"

Scottie glanced at Konrad, catching a furrow at his brow. He answered less casually, sharper and more professional. "This is Scottie Roberts. She's my temp while Marisol is out."

"Right." Jeff's gaze was fixed on her. He offered his large palm to her. "Nice to meet you, Scottie. I'm Jeff—"

"The sneaky bastard," she said, finishing for him. "Yeah, I heard." She took his hand, the heat of their contact making her feel woozy. Or maybe it was because Konrad had suddenly become very interested in her every move.

Jeff laughed heartily. "I like her."

"Yes." Konrad's one word was a bit clipped. "That is obvious."

If Scottie didn't know better, she'd think Konrad had an issue with the way Jeff looked at her. Because he *did* have a hint of interest dancing in his eyes. The way Konrad had looked at her at the dinner party.

Scottie said, "I'm taking the grand tour of Korr Solutions."

"Cool." Jeff didn't stop flirting, though Konrad's objection to it was clear. He continued, "Want me to show her around, Kon?"

"No, I've got this under control, thank you, Jeff." Again, his hand pressed against Scottie's back to push her in the opposite direction. That time, however, she didn't jump away from him.

"No worries. Oh, hey, it was nice to meet you, Scottie."

Scottie pulled her attention from Konrad, which was no little feat considering the heat of his hand burned her flesh. She was breathless. Stumbling over her words, she said, "Nice to meet you too, Jeff."

Jeff didn't walk away, though, but hesitated. Then he said to Scottie, "So, every Thursday the software team goes to happy hour at Bowie Brew a couple of blocks from here. Want to join us?"

She glanced at Konrad, who didn't hide his emotions about that. And he also didn't remove his hand, which had been on her too long to not be noticed.

Why would he hate the idea of her joining Jeff for happy hour? It shouldn't matter. She didn't need his approval. He didn't control what she did after work hours. In fact, she wasn't his to control, period. He had enough women under his control.

Scottie stepped forward, Konrad's hand falling from her back, leaving her abandoned without his touch. But it needed to be done. She lifted her chin in silent defiance. "Sure. Sounds fun."

"Already trying to corrupt my temp, Jeff?" Konrad likely said it in jest, but there was no humor underneath.

Jeff grinned, seeming triumphant. "That's not part of my job description."

"No, it's not. Now get back to what is your job description." Konrad practically shoved Scottie until they were halfway down the corridor.

"He seems nice."

Konrad grunted. They turned yet another corner of the ice-cold labyrinth of the suite. "Here is where the data magic happens. This is the software engineering department. Out of curiosity, do you have any coding experience? I know some BBA programs require a computer science credit."

"Uh…" Scottie had to get her bearings. He was distant again. Nothing like he was seconds ago. "I took two semesters of software development in college, so I do understand how to write and read basic code."

"Excellent. We lost someone this morning, and we are a bit shorthanded. I may have you do some software debugging."

And just like that, he went back to not caring about what she did.

The rest of the afternoon flew by without much from Konrad, who'd shut himself in his office. Scottie busied herself with ordering lunch for some upcoming meetings later in the week. Also, she'd received an email from Anisette, thanking Konrad for the Chanel scarf. She didn't seem as pissed off as Tamsin. Maybe he was being ethical in telling the women what they were getting themselves into?

Scottie wondered where Pilar was in all this. She also wondered if she could theoretically agree to his conditions of non-commitment, to have him just for a night. The thought jolted her to reality. No. A casual thing wasn't her game. She needed all or nothing from a man.

Chapter Seven

Wednesday morning, on a whim, Konrad decided to take Scottie on a field trip to see the EaDo property. He'd completely ignored the fact that he'd never taken Marisol to see it or any other property since he'd set up his headquarters in Houston earlier in the year. He hoped everyone else would ignore that fact too.

Unlike his typical office attire, he dressed casually in worn jeans, a white button-up shirt with the sleeves rolled to his elbows, and casual Prada shoes. Employees would raise their brows because he'd always worn a suit to work. It was his armor.

"Dress for the level of success you want," his father always said to him. Konrad had not been a stranger to three-piece suits in boarding school and beyond. Perfectly tailored. Perfectly put together. His father insisted on it. Image was always important to him. Konrad too.

Susan wasn't at her desk when he walked through the lobby before eight in the morning. Scottie, on the other hand, sat at her desk drinking coffee from his favorite Harvard coffee mug. It had gone missing the day before. When he saw her perfect lips latch onto the rim, though, all he could think about was how those lips would look on him. If he didn't have such great self-control, he would have been hard with the thought.

For fuck's sake.

He cleared his throat. "Good morning, Scottie."

Startled, her eyes jerked up to his from her sitting position. She dropped the cup from her lips and sat it on the desk, then swallowed, making Konrad really have to get control of himself, and said, "Good morning, Konrad."

His gaze fell to her simple black flats as she sat crossed-legged, her toes pointed to him. She'd worn a pair of cropped trousers and a striped shirt. Very French. Finally, an outfit he liked, not including the black skirt he hadn't been able to stop musing about. Legs like hers should be shown often. Daily. Nightly… *My God.*

"I'm glad you're wearing flat shoes today." His eyes lingered over her ankles too long. Scottie surely noticed. "I'm taking you on a road trip. Can you be ready in fifteen minutes?"

Her cheeks flushed. "Where are we going?"

"To visit the infamous EaDo property."

She hesitated. "Who else is going?"

A slow smile pulled his lips. "Just us."

Gulping hard, she asked, "Just us?"

"You're not scared, are you?" He should not have asked that. A-Plus Temporaries would cancel their contract if they knew how unprofessional he'd been with her since she'd stepped foot in his office. She liked it though. Had to. If not, she'd be gone on her own accord.

Scottie frowned with indignation. "No."

"Excellent." He spun on his heels toward his office, gratified to see her still watching him in the reflection of his glass door. Over his shoulder, he said, "Be ready in fifteen, yeah?"

Not waiting for a response, he entered his office and let the lock catch before he exhaled. He sat at his desk, musing about how damned lucky his Harvard mug was.

The feeling didn't last long enough. The ring of his cell phone quelled the lightness he felt about taking Scottie out of the office alone. Tamsin's face flashed on the screen. Didn't the blow-off flowers say it all? Then again, he needed to remember who he was dealing with, although he just wanted to forget. Impossible, though.

She wasn't going to let it go, and he needed to face her. And his actions.

He groaned, letting it ring three times before he answered. "Tamsin." He stood and walked to the picturesque window. Staring out, he waited for her hard breathing to turn into words.

"I don't appreciate the kiss-off, Konrad." She was irate and ready for a fight. Another one.

He drew in a long sigh. "You're right. It was a kiss-off."

Pausing for a moment, he could hear her surprise. "So you admit it then?"

God, she was such a lawyer. When had he not been on trial with her? "Guilty."

Another few beats passed. "I'm willing to overlook this and figure out an arrangement we both agree on."

He groaned inside. Everything was up for interpretation to her. But the truth was, she simply didn't take rejection well. Unfortunately, that wasn't open to interpretation. Their ending was inevitable. It baffled Konrad that she didn't see it coming. Nonetheless, he had to be delicate. He had to make her see she didn't really want him. She wanted the power to be the ender, not the endee. That was *her* game.

"I see other women, Tamsin. I date women regularly. I said this to you when we first got together."

"You mean when we first fucked at your mate's hotel?" she said, practically choking on her question.

"Let's not make this obscene, Tammy." He raked a hand through his hair, remembering that night he met her at the Mariposa bar at Halman Hotel. "I want to be honest with you."

Her voice softened. "I want that, too."

"Please don't take this personally. I think you're

smashing. Truly. I've had amazing fun with you, but we don't want the same thing anymore. You clearly want a commitment, and I think you should have your heart's desires."

"And I can't be your desire?" Tamsin's urgency made his stomach flip.

Damn. This was hard. "Not the way you want."

Konrad had never heard himself speak so openly before. He'd never had a breakup talk like that. The discomfort was unavoidable, but something deeper within felt satisfied. "Look, I know you think you want me, but you don't. There are plenty of blokes who would love to have a go with you. I just don't want a go with anyone. I need to be free."

The words seemed right, but the feeling wasn't anymore. He wanted a go with someone. He wanted to feel what it was like to connect on a deeper level, to feel out of control for someone. Like what Fabian had with Antonia.

Tamsin was rendered speechless, which was a first.

"Tamsin, love," he said, his voice steady. "I really think you'll thank me later."

She didn't respond. The only response was the silent line. She'd hung up. She didn't even say goodbye, but Konrad knew it was goodbye.

He took five extra minutes staring out into the Houston sky after his conversation. He'd felt empty inside. No way could he deny he wasn't affected. In the past, he'd dumped women and had felt exhilarated, ready to meet another. Because there was always another. Women were everywhere, ready to fall into his bed. But he didn't feel exhilarated and ready to meet another. Quite the opposite. Instead, he wondered what he would do with Anisette and Pilar.

Twenty minutes later, he tapped on Scottie's cube wall.

"You're late," she said, her mouth curled in a smirk.

"I can be late. I'm the boss." He winked.

She shook her head in disapproval. "Do as I say, not as I do, huh?"

Bold. His excitement bubbled up inside. She moved him more than he ever could have expected. "And when did I say that, Miss Roberts?"

She pursed her lips together, repressing a smile. "Fine. You didn't say that."

Blood coursed through his veins at lightning speed. Without fail, his attraction to her grew every second. "Now that we've settled that, come on." He turned from her cube, his eyelids closing for a second.

Konrad honestly didn't know if she followed him until he'd reached the lobby and stopped at Susan's desk. Then he realized Scottie was so close behind him he could feel her heat, smell her sweet perfume.

"We're going out for a bit."

Susan's gaze slid from Konrad's to Scottie's and then back to Konrad. "Oh?"

"I'm taking Scottie to the EaDo property this morning. We'll be back after lunch." A minor detail he didn't mention to Scottie.

Susan narrowed her eyes but quickly became distracted by an incoming call. He waved to her and turned to Scottie.

"Off we go."

Ten minutes later, he held open the passenger side door of his coupe for her. Scottie slipped in.

"This is your car?" She looked like she'd sucked on a lemon.

He chuckled. "Do you not like it?"

She glanced inside, her gaze moving over all his upgraded features and custom finishes. She snorted low. "What's not to like?"

He closed the door to the car but wanted to throw open the door to her life. Who was she? Where was she from? Why had she reacted to him the way she had?

Once he'd settled into the driver's seat where he belonged, he turned on the engine, reveling in the sound. The beauty of the machine woke up for him as he commanded. His cars were his unabated love. Escaping in them, down the road to anywhere, was a regular joy. Konrad had a total of four cars, but Scottie didn't need to know that. Yet.

Scottie crossed her arms as well as her legs. Gazing out the passenger window, she didn't give him a single clue as to what was on her mind. At times, she'd been too hard to read, even when they were face-to-face. He needed to know, did she like him? Did she trust him, even if just a little? They'd met only days ago, but their close proximity made him feel they'd been acquainted longer.

Konrad put the car in "reverse," glancing at her before he set his eyes on the navigation screen. "Don't worry. I'm a fantastic driver." From his periphery, he saw her glance at him. At that, he smiled, though small. Something was between them. He was acutely aware of how their energies played. In the small space, it was impossible not to feel it.

Once on the road for a few miles, just as they were leaving downtown proper, she uncrossed her arms, her hands falling on her lap. He wanted to press his hand against her thigh, get her attention. Attention had come to him without fail from anyone he wanted it from, yet she left him wanting hers. The need was disturbing to him, making him feel a desperation he didn't know how to reconcile.

"You're quiet, Scottine."

"Scottie," she corrected.

"Sorry. Scottie." He chuckled to himself. "I don't know why you don't like Scottine. It's a gorgeous name." *Gorgeous*. He seemed to struggle to pick his words carefully when he spoke to her casually. But her name *was* gorgeous. Just like her. He turned his gaze to her thigh again, wishing she'd worn the black skirt.

She caught his stare, and quickly he turned back to the road. She stumbled over her words. "Who said I didn't like Scottine?"

"I just assumed."

"Well, you know what happens when you assume." Humor laced her voice, and he liked how it sounded on her lips.

"Indeed, I do." They came to a stop sign. With his eyes still on the red circular light overhead, he asked, "Is Scottine a family name?"

"It's my father's name. Well, his name is William *Scott* Roberts." Her voice lowered, as though she were talking to herself. "God only knows why my mom wanted to name me after him."

Frozen, without a response, he waited for her, but she didn't continue. A tug in his heart made him feel for her. It was the most profound information she'd offered, and it was so private and intimate. He knew he didn't deserve it, although he was honored to hear it. In that sharing moment, of her opening her door a little, he worried he'd mess it up. For that he let the light turn green and stepped on the gas again. Not another word for minutes.

"Tell me more about yourself." He took the initiative, hoping it wasn't too soon.

She hesitated. "Well … I went to the University

of Houston. Studied Business Administration—"

"Tell me something I can't find on your résumé." He laughed, trying to lighten the mood.

She stalled. "Uhh… I think your accent is strange."

With a chortle, he said, "Thank you. I think."

She laughed, a lovely sound. "Why is it so strange? Where are you really from? Mars?"

He chuckled, though she didn't. "I suppose because I lived in more than one place. And I have been everywhere."

"That's vague."

His laugh has louder, from his belly. He loved their banter. "I'm German born but was educated in the UK and in France for a little while."

"You speak French?" She seemed impressed, finally. And he wanted her to always sound that way around him.

"*Oui, mademoiselle.*"

A sigh fell from her lips, loud enough for him to hear, and it sent chills down his spine.

"And you speak German, too?"

"That's my mother tongue, *Schatzi.*" He should not have said *tongue* to her. "And I speak other languages, too."

"What's *Schatzi* mean?"

He stalled, not wanting to explain. *Schatzi* meant *sweetie* in German. That was inappropriate. But, hell, he couldn't help himself. "It's a German term of endearment…"

She turned to face him, and from his periphery, he saw she'd lifted her eyebrows. "Oh." She turned again, and he was glad she'd seemed to let it go. "Do you speak Spanish?"

"A little. Do you?"

She scoffed. "Yes."

They were silent for a while, the moving cars and city noises muffled by the windows. But she broke that silence just when he thought she was done talking.

"No wonder you have to send flowers to all those women."

The meaning sobered him. To Scottie, he was a rich player who had his way with women and threw them away. She'd never as much said the words, but he knew that was what she thought about him. And he hated it enough to feel the anger at the unfairness of her words. He wanted her to see the real man behind her first impressions.

"How do you mean?" he asked in response to her comment, his jaw clenched.

"Women like accents. And guys who speak multiple languages."

His heart thumped so hard, he felt his chest against the seat belt. "So I've heard." *Do you like that too?*

Scottie crossed her arms again and didn't say another word until they reached the EaDo property. And though he desperately wanted to continue the conversation, he didn't. He'd have to remember he was her boss, and this conversation probably shouldn't go any further, despite what he wanted.

Chapter Eight

Scottie knew she was pushing it with Konrad. He was her boss. Her *boss*. Even if her temporary boss. A-Plus Temporaries wouldn't like how she acted in their name. She was their representative, and she'd been so unprofessional. She should be fired.

She was so moved by him, though. Wasn't that enough justification for her behavior?

Konrad parked his ridiculously gorgeous Mercedes along the side of a long metal building on a massive lot at the edge of east downtown. A huge sign at the wired fence read *Korr Properties*. She didn't even want to begin to think about how rich Konrad was.

To her surprise, the building on the inside wasn't as industrial and drab as a typical warehouse would be. It was steel and stone and very chic. No question why there was a bidding war for the warehouse.

"Wow. This is actually beautiful." Scottie felt tiny in the immense room.

His sigh tickled her ears, made her tingle. "It is." He turned to her for a moment. "I like beautiful things."

Konrad winked, making her insides tremble. God, how could she stay professional when he did things like that? When he irked her in so many ways and aroused her in others? But, she'd seen him with other employees, like the way he'd been with Sandy the receptionist. It was his personality. After three days, it was absurd that Scottie fought this battle inside herself. What would it be like after working three months for Konrad? If she lasted that long…

They walked the length of the building, covering every inch of the property. The grandeur of it took her breath away. Once they were back outside, they surveyed the lot, which contrasted with the pure art of the interior. The property was properly situated among other nearby warehouses and manufacturing plants, which were nothing like Konrad's building. Lost in her thoughts of Konrad and the style she'd seen emerge in all that he owned, she stared at his profile. He looked out into the lot, sunglasses on his face. Everything about him was perfectly proportioned. Everything about him was aesthetic, like the gorgeous art he had in all his offices. In that moment, he wasn't the playboy boss, he was something to admire.

Suddenly, he turned, seemingly becoming aware of her staring, musing. He took off his sunglasses, meeting her gaze that didn't falter, though it should have. His blue to her hazel, their eyes fused in some understanding that evaded her. But, dear God, she wanted him to lean down and kiss her more than she wanted anything else, despite what she knew about him.

She gasped, caught in her emotions. "Why did you bring me here?"

A languid and provocative curl formed over his lips. "I wanted you to see what drives me."

Somehow, with some energy reserve she had deep inside, she forced her eyes from him and back to the expanse of the gravelly lot. "Selling property?"

"Seeing my name on something big like this."

Their eyes met again. Was he making a point? To himself? To others?

"Well, there is no mistaking who owns this, that's for sure." Knowing fully the power this man had over everything in his life made her breathless.

She couldn't help but wonder: what else did he want to own? A ripple moved through her body, concentrating at the apex of her thighs. Though against everything she believed, she wanted to be owned by him, even if for just the seconds they stood there together.

In a soft voice, he said, "No, there isn't."

Under the weight of his stare, she felt feather light. Like she was floating over the gravelly ground. He moved in on her, and she gulped down hard. *Oh God.*

His hand came up, brushing against her cheek. She didn't step back. Breath puffed between her lips. This was it. He was going to kiss her.

But then he pulled his hand back, his index finger pointed. "Make a wish."

Discombobulated and intoxicated with being so close to him, she didn't know how to respond. She didn't really understand what he said at first. "What?"

"It's an eyelash." His smile made her weak. With the slow and languid seduction he always possessed, he licked his bottom lip. "Make a wish."

Reality came fast, and the notion that he would kiss her was over. "Oh."

He furrowed his brow. "Don't you have a wish?"

Yes. And it was not going to happen. "Of course."

"Then blow."

Her eyes snapped to his, her body alive with wanting him. God, she wanted to blow. And she wanted to do more stupid things with this man. With this boss of hers. But then he dropped his hand, his gaze steady on hers. Without thinking, and completely forgetting who they were to each other, she lifted on her toes and pressed her mouth against his. His arms circled her immediately, drawing her closer into his large body. She moaned, taking his lip between hers. When his tongue met hers, she pushed away.

Oh God no.

Embarrassment made her hot enough to combust. She turned away from him. No way could she look into his eyes.

"I'm sorry." Her fingers went to her mouth. "I don't know why I did that."

"No, it's okay." His warm hand touched her back.

"God, this is so embarrassing." A wiggle of her body made his hand fall away. "The agency would fire me—"

"Don't worry." He touched her again. "I wanted— I—" He clamped his lips in a firm line as he paused. "I won't let the agency punish you for what we both wanted."

She didn't look at him, didn't say another word. What was there to say? The desire she had building inside since she met him came forth in the worst way.

"Scottine, look at me, please."

She had to get out of there. Now. If she looked at him, she didn't know what would happen. Moving toward the shiny car, she opened the passenger door. "We should get back. I'm not up for lunch."

It was over. And she hoped the kiss would be forgotten.

Chapter Nine

Konrad thought of one thing and one thing only, even as he sat across from Pilar at L'Atelier for dinner that night. The kiss with Scottie. God, her lips. Her fucking lips… He wanted another chance to really show her what he could do. Did she regret it? If she did, it would gut him. *For fuck's sake, what the hell is happening to me?* His stomach was in knots. A woman had never completely taken up his mind like this.

Pilar's fork dropping on her plate caught his attention. "You're far away," she said.

"I know, love. Sorry." He'd hardly touched his scallops, and they were his favorite.

"Is it work?" She leaned in, her low-plunging top framing her breasts perfectly. He gazed at them for a second, but, for the first time, didn't feel desire to touch them, lick them. Put them in his mouth. Or any of the other things he'd done to them.

"Sort of," he finally answered. Scottie was his temp, so technically it was work.

It was so much more than that, though. Also for the first time, he felt dissatisfied with his life. Not his businesses. They were growing faster than projected. Professionally, he was golden. Socially, he was very satisfied. His couldn't ask for better mates. It was something else. It was personal. He'd felt lonely. After seeing Fabian and the change that reformed him into a new person, Konrad had this newborn desire to want something more than a rotation of women. He wanted what Fabian had, and that desire had come on quick, strong. Unbearably so. But when Scottie kissed him, he didn't feel that longing. He felt excitement and a yearning that stayed with him even after she avoided him the rest of the day.

Pilar tilted her head, her gaze soft on his, waiting for more from him. "Tell me."

An interruption saved him from having to say words out loud that he wasn't ready to. He and Pilar turned their attention to the person standing at the table.

"Pilly," a good-looking, well-dressed man said in accusation. He was younger than Konrad, and he didn't look pleased. "I didn't know you'd be here."

Pilar glanced at Konrad, her eyebrows quirked. "I told you I had plans tonight."

Konrad wanted to laugh. Obviously, this guy was on Pilar's rotation. Leaning back in his chair, he felt an odd sense of relief at the turn of events.

"Who's this?" the man asked, not looking at Konrad but pointing a finger at him.

Konrad didn't care for that but let it go. This wasn't his fight.

Pilar slapped down his pointed finger. "Esteban, this is my friend Konrad. Konrad, this is my other friend Esteban."

"Other friend?" Esteban wasn't impressed.

Konrad didn't chuckle that time, gaining a pointed looked from the shafted Esteban.

"Yes." She didn't blink an eye. Good God, she was just like him. Konrad knew that tone. That look in her eyes. That dare-to-defy-and-you'll-be-gone attitude. That was him.

"Nice to meet you," Konrad said, holding his hand out.

Esteban ignored Konrad, which made Pilar even more furious. "You're being very rude, Esteban."

With panic tangling his voice, he demanded, "So what we talked about last night didn't mean anything?"

Konrad felt bad for Esteban. His heart twisted

with the display of emotion, but he wondered if he could ever show that kind of emotion. If he could make a complete ass of himself for someone. There was a freedom in it that Konrad never considered before. In fact, he'd always considered it bondage.

Pilar stood. "Excuse me just a moment, Konrad."

Konrad leaned back in his chair. "Of course." He watched them leave the table as he drank from his short glass of scotch. Immediately, he thought about Scottie again, wondering if she would show up to work the next day. He hoped to God she would.

After dinner, Konrad drove Pilar back to her private on-campus apartment for international students. She'd been silent instead of her usual talkative self. He parked and faced her, taking in the light catching her blue-black hair. Pilar's eyes were dark like onyxes, but all he could see were Scottie's hazel irises the second before his assistant put her lips on his.

"Are you okay?" she asked, taking him from his thoughts.

Konrad turned off the music. He needed to think about what he intended to say, how he intended to tell Pilar what their future would look like. "Yes. Are you okay?"

"I'm sorry about Esteban." She sighed in exasperation. "He's so persistent and needy."

"Looks like it."

"He'll get over it." She pushed her hair over her one shoulder and smiled at him. He knew that smile. It was her come-to-my-room smile. But he wouldn't go in that time.

He couldn't.

"I didn't get to really talk to you." He glanced down at her legs.

She uncrossed them, knees shifting in his

direction. "I know." Her eyebrows arched the more she focused on his face. "You aren't okay, are you? Is it because I met your friends the other night?"

He shook his head. "No. It's not that."

Her fingers moved over the console to touch his thigh. When he didn't touch her back, she pulled away, a frown on her face. "What is it? Tell me."

He struggled for the words simply because he'd never had to describe these feelings he was having before. "I'm going through something, Pilly. I don't know. I need to pull away for a little while." Or forever. He wasn't sure.

"You don't want to see me anymore?" Her eyes widened, but she wasn't emotional the way Tamsin had been.

"I do want to. But not in the same way as before." The struggle got to him. For the first time, he was raw in front of someone. "I need to put all this to a halt and figure out some stuff in my life. I still want to talk to you, though. I mean, if you still want to talk to me."

Silence infiltrated the cabin. Not awkward though. It was light and comforting.

"Is it someone else? It's okay. You can tell me."

"No... I don't know." He shook his head. He could not stop thinking about Scottie. About their time together at the EaDo property. The kiss. He could not stop thinking about how much he wanted her, wanted to kiss her again.

"It's okay, *guapo*. I understand." She leaned in and kissed his cheek.

Before he knew it, she opened the door and closed it, leaving him alone in his car with just his thoughts. And all his thoughts were about Scottie.

Chapter Ten

Scottie didn't see Konrad on Thursday morning, and she'd had her eye on his door, waiting for him. He hadn't come in the office. Would he? It wasn't until the afternoon when she received an email from him. He'd be visiting other Korr properties for the rest of the day. So, she'd have to wait longer to see him again. All for the better. Had to be. She shouldn't be waiting for him in anticipation, thinking of the way she threw herself at him in her one moment of weakness. But he was such a good kisser. The kiss consumed her. She'd not kissed a guy in at least a year. Probably more. Damn, she felt so off balance thinking about him, wondering what would have happened had she not pulled away.

Later that day, a few minutes before five, he returned to the office, not saying single word to her as he stomped to his office. Not even a hello. Fine by her. Something affected him. Nothing she needed to worry about. If anything, she needed to get him off her mind for good. What transpired between them was a mistake. A stupid, thoughtless mistake. She needed to forget it and focus on her work. The temp position would be over soon, and, she hoped, she'd have a permanent job elsewhere. Away from Konrad.

Scottie was warm. Too many thoughts roiled in her head. God, this whole forgetting what happened wasn't working out. *Give it a day.* That seemed like too long. Just as she was about to glance in Konrad's office, her office phone rang, making her jump with the loud buzz. Scottie looked at the caller ID screen mounted on the top. It was Jeff from Korr Solutions. She'd forgotten about the weekly happy hour. With the way she'd been feeling, she badly needed a drink.

Scottie picked up the receiver. "Hey, Jeff."

A force beyond her control made her gaze drift to Konrad's office. A piercing pair of blue eyes startled her from across the aisle. He stared at her, a furrow at his brow, making her heart skip. *God, he is beautiful.*

"Are you still coming to happy hour? We're about to walk over."

"Uhh … yes, of course." She shifted her gaze back to the phone, her heart still skipping and making her breathless.

"Meet us in the lobby." Jeff was ecstatic, and Scottie wish she could feel the same enthusiasm for him. She really just wanted the adult beverage to get her mind off her life.

It would be cool if Konrad joins us. The thought came upon her so quickly. *You're an idiot, Scottie.* A drink with him would be a bad idea.

"I'm leaving now," she said, wanting to get out from under Konrad's pull on her.

Scottie gathered her things to leave after she hung up. Stepping out of her cube, Konrad surprised her. He stood near her desk, a folder in his grip. Her hand flew to her chest, covering her wildly beating heart. "You scared me!"

"You're so skittish, Scottie."

She glowered. "You do like to sneak up on people, don't you?"

A smile was his response. She could only imagine what he was thinking, and it made her avert her gaze from his curled-up, sexy-as-hell lips. Lips she'd kissed.

Oh God.

"So where are you off to, then?"

None of your business. She relented. "Bowie Brew for the coworker happy hour."

Konrad's eyes grew darker. Smile gone. "Did you

see my response about Anisette's thank-you card?"

Don't roll your eyes. Don't roll your eyes. Player Konrad was back. The Player Konrad who needed Scottie to manage his women, which she was tired of doing.

"Yes. I emailed her a response to her thank-you." *Now turn around and walk away.*

"Brilliant."

He said nothing more, yet didn't leave.

"Okay … well, they're waiting for me in the lobby." She half turned away. "Unless there is anything else you need from me…"

Scottie's frustration grew exponentially. But it was toward herself, not him. After their trip to the EaDo property, she should stop thinking they could be familiar with each other. As if the kiss changed anything between them. It didn't. They still only had a professional relationship. If only her body could get on board with her brain.

"No. I don't need anything else from you."

Of course not. She didn't need anything else from him either.

Chapter Eleven

Go see her. No, I can't.

Those statements dueled in Konrad's mind for at least a half an hour after Scottie left, leaving a trail of her sugary perfume behind. The faint smell remained in his car, and he savored it until it left. He must've been hooked if he was savoring her perfume as if it were an IV giving him energy. But there he was doing it. Decision made. He wanted to smell her perfume again.

Screw the Thursday happy hour he'd had with his mates every week. Konrad needed to see Scottie again. Out of the office. He needed to be close to her. Maybe nothing would happen. It didn't matter. He just wanted to be near her.

An email notification chimed his computer just as he was about to leave. He glanced at it, annoyed to be kept any longer. Fabian had sent him a link to the *Houston Society Pages* engagement announcements. Front and center was a picture of Fabian and Antonia, smiling like fools. A caption underneath it read: *Two powerhouse families unite with the engagement of Antonia Robuchon to Fabian Pallis.*

The same dense, dull feeling Konrad had at their surprise engagement dinner came back full force. Oh God, could it be possible Konrad's feelings had progressed to outright jealousy of their engagement? That he himself wanted to have exactly what they had?

His gaze drifted to the announcement below. Shocked at first, he looked away just to be sure his eyes weren't playing tricks on him. He read the announcement again.

Houston socialite Anisette Bonnenfont and real estate mogul Blaine Craft announced their engagement among family and close friends last night at an intimate dinner. They plan a Turks and Caicos destination wedding next spring.

Blimey. Was everyone getting married?

Konrad sat back in his chair. His mind spun with the news. He didn't know she had been dating someone else. Good on her. Anisette deserved a real estate mogul who could give her forever. He was sure that was why she'd visited him, to tell him she wasn't available for anymore dalliances, for the convenient get-togethers he'd demanded of all his women. And he'd ditched her. Sent her a Chanel scarf instead.

Fuck, Korr, you're a real tosser. No more. He didn't want to be that anymore.

He looked up from his computer, staring at Scottie's cube through the glass wall. His obligations were gone. All the women he'd been seeing, he'd either pushed them away or they'd left him. The slate was clean again.

He looked back at the announcement on his computer screen and wondered what it would be like to read his own engagement announcement. Konrad shut his laptop, his body soaring to get to Scottie.

The moment Konrad stepped foot in the Bowie Brew, he got a whiff of cheap liquor. He may as well have sniffed a bottle of rubbing alcohol. Never would he be caught dead in a dive bar, but this wasn't about appearances. He was there for something that might be a terrible idea.

A rowdy group at the far end of the bar caught his attention. *His* group. They carried on with drinks in their grips. Scottie was the one who laughed the loudest, which brought a smile to his face. He wished she laughed more around him. She had no idea how beautiful she looked when she laughed. He approached, noticing

Scottie held a beer. He'd not pegged her for a beer girl. She looked more like a fruity type. Fuzzy navel maybe. Or sex on the beach. Images popped in his head about sex on the beach. With her.

His body responded to the images, and he had to stop his stride for a second to contain himself. Then, warm and zipping with energy, he moved again toward the group, wondering if she would still be calm as if nothing had happened between them, as if they didn't share secrets. He must have sent out telekinetic messages to her, because she turned her gaze to his, her eyes widening from the surprise. It wasn't exactly an indication she was happy to see him, and it made him wonder if he had been too presumptuous. Did the kiss affect her at all? But then a small smile curled her lips, and he was energized again.

Konrad approached the group, smiling with each acknowledgement of his employees.

"Well, look who's graced us with his presence. The boss man himself." Jeff's voice boomed over the loud bar. He might have already had one drink too many.

Konrad bowed to an awkward applause, and when he stood to his full height, he noticed Scottie's eyes on him. Light flashed in her olive irises, making him think she might be happy to see him. "I just wanted to make sure my employees are not terrorizing anyone in my name."

"Never!" Jeff said, deceitfully joyful. There was no mistake he wasn't enthused with Konrad's presence. "Have a seat."

An empty seat beside Scottie beckoned Konrad. He pointed to it. "That chair has my name on it." All eyes were on him as he squeezed between Scottie and the empty chair, his hand touching her arm in the process. "Pardon me."

His heart pounding, he leaned into Scottie, getting a whiff of her perfume, and peered at her glass. "What are you drinking?" he asked.

"Uhh…" She seemed bothered but didn't back away from him. "It's pear ale."

He chuckled. "I didn't take you for a pear ale type of person."

Her eyebrows quirked up, eyes glittering. "Oh really? What type of person did you take me for?"

Don't say, "Sex on the beach." "I don't know. Something fruity."

"Fruity?" She was amused with his assessment.

"Right. Like … a fuzzy navel or something so dreadful as that." He laughed, and to his surprise, she did too.

"I most certainly am not a fuzzy navel drinker."

"That's excellent. You can keep your job then." Konrad winked at her, but it was the heavy silence around the table that pulled his attention back to his employees. They'd caught Konrad flirting with Scottie, because that was exactly what he'd done.

"And what kind of person are *you*, boss man? Let me guess, schnapps?" Jeff stared at Konrad, straight and unwavering. If Konrad didn't know better, Jeff had challenged him to a duel of sorts.

The group snickered a little in the awkwardness that blanketed the table.

"Very clever, Jeff." Waggling his finger, he lifted it to his temple.

"Why is that clever?" asked one of his female software engineers, probably completely lost to what was going on—just as everyone else.

Konrad held Jeff's gaze. This was a duel. "It's a German drink, you see. But, I didn't learn to drink in Germany."

"Where did you learn?" Jeff's blatant defiance was getting under Konrad's skin.

"Scotland." A smile pulled at Konrad's face. "Are you surprised?"

Jeff winked at Scottie, and it was clear what the challenge was for. "Scotch. Very classy."

"I like scotch," Scottie offered, glancing at Konrad. She seemed uncomfortable.

"Let's get a glass, then?" Jeff's eyebrows raised, his attention on Scottie. "Your first round is on me, boss."

"I assume you're using your corporate card to pay for all the rounds." The group laughed. "So all rounds on me." *Checkmate*. Konrad was the boss, and he would not be shown up by anyone.

Jeff lifted his hands in defeat. "You got me there." He touched Scottie's hand from across the table, all eyes on the action. "Come with me to the bar."

Konrad burned with the need to push Jeff's fingers off hers.

Scottie stood, hitting Konrad's arm. "Sure." Their touch sparked Konrad straight to his chest. Before she wiggled her way from the chair, she leaned toward Konrad. "Which one do you want?"

Their eyes lingered, danced. He wanted to lean in the few inches they were apart and kiss her. "Surprise me."

A small smiled curved her lips for a brief moment, and Konrad thought he might be the victor after all. "Okay."

Konrad watched them leave. Something had happened between them in those moments. The same thing that had happened out on his property and when they kissed. No denying it. His feeling was spot on.

Employee after employee commented on his

presence. They were surprised. Glad he joined them. Thought it was cool to have a drink with the boss. Konrad nodded. If only they knew why he was really there. He tried to stay entertained by them, but his attention kept shifting back to the bar. Jeff stood a bit too close to Scottie, and at one point, Jeff leaned over to say something in Scottie's ear.

Konrad had to force himself to stay calm, indifferent. His employees couldn't know what he was thinking about, or more specifically, who.

"Who knows, clan. I may join you all from now on." Not bloody likely. He'd no intention on setting foot in the Bowie Brew ever again. If he was so lucky to take Scottie for a drink, it would be at a place with white table cloths and crystal.

Relief hit him once Scottie and Jeff returned, each holding multiple drinks. Upon sitting, she handed him a glass. He didn't want to think what year the scotch was or how horrible it probably tasted. The only scotch he liked could not be bought in a place like the Bowie Brew.

"I hope you like it," she said apologetically, her tone smooth in his ear.

"I'm sure it's fine." The glass nearly slipped between his fingers.

"It was the best they had that your money could buy," Jeff chimed in. Everyone laughed again.

"I appreciate it, Jeff."

Scottie sat, bumping Konrad. Settled, she lifted her glass to him. "Well, cheers."

"Wait, wait…" Jeff interjected, ruining Konrad and Scottie's moment. Everyone silenced, waiting for him to continue. He held up his glass, his eyes set on Konrad. "I want to make a toast. To the boss, Mr. Korr—"

"Lord Korr." Konrad winked at Scottie, who

lifted her fingers to her plump lips, hiding a grin. A burst of laughter followed.

"Right. Lord Korr." Jeff continued. "What other boss would join his employees for a drink in a dive bar? To the most fair, talented, and ethical boss I've ever had. Thank you."

Ethical boss was the only thing Konrad heard. Jeff clearly had a position to state, and it wasn't the compliment he'd offered.

"Well, it's not just me on this team. It's all of you. It's the whole Korr Corp—Solutions and Properties—that make us successful. All my fair, talented, and *ethical* employees. So, thank *you*." Before Konrad could gauge Jeff's reaction, his phone vibrated in his pocket.

Everyone else clicked glasses, except Konrad, who turned his attention to his phone screen.

Dallas Halman: **630, Korr. Where the hell are you?**

He'd never missed a guys' dinner since he arrived in Houston not quite two years ago.

Me: **Having a drink with my employees. Catch you blokes next time!**

That did not go over well.

Dallas Halman: **You're what?**

Another text vibrated his phone.

Fabian P: **Get your ass to L'Atelier.**

Then another.

Ty Westmore: **Explain yourself.**

Annoying wankers. He sent a group message.

Me: **Get off my back. I'm working on my employees' morale for fuck's sake.**

Dallas Halman: **sure you are...**

Me: **Goodnight, gentlemen.**

Konrad turned off the phone completely, and he

hoped Dallas would keep his mouth shut about Scottie. A lot had happened since he'd talked about her, and he'd hate Dallas to cheapen the feelings Konrad now had. One thing was for sure, he would not talk about her again to any of his friends until there was something to talk about.

"Scottie, have you been a temp for long?" Jeff's question caught Konrad's attention.

She looked up from her sip of scotch. Embarrassed, or ambivalent, she hesitated. "Uhh … no, not long. I just graduated from college in May." She glanced around the table, all eyes on her. "This actually is my first assignment as a temp."

Her first … assignment. He liked the notion of being a first to her.

Another software engineer asked, "What do you do for fun? Besides drink with coworkers."

Scottie laughed nervously, clearly hating the attention that had been focused on her. "Oh, nothing exciting." She took another sip, gaze down inside her glass.

The group silenced, and when Scottie didn't say any more, they resumed other conversations.

In a voice low enough for her ears but not the others', Konrad said, "Oh, come on, Scottine, you must live an exciting life."

Her gorgeous hazel eyes lifted to meet his. A small smile on her lips. "Just read the extracurricular activities section on my résumé." Then she grew serious. "But I'm sure it's not as exciting as your life. You have been everywhere, after all. And you have everything you want, it seems."

The comment wasn't complimentary. It hurt. Were they back to that? He wasn't sure. Konrad took her in, the straightened lips, the darkened eyes. The slight flush on her face to suggest she knew she went too far.

She had, but maybe he deserved it. "Don't be so sure about that."

Chapter Twelve

Too many thoughts ran through Scottie's head, none coherent. None gave her clarity. Konrad had definitely been rivaling with Jeff. The whole table knew it. Was the fight for her?

After their kiss, she wasn't sure what to expect from Konrad. Even though she'd started the kiss, she'd ended it. It was a mistake, and she still felt that it was. But the more she looked at him and felt his dynamism take her, she wasn't as sure anymore. Scottie needed to stop presuming to know him. *Was* his life exciting? *Did* he have everything he wanted? She didn't have a clue. His expression said it all. She was the asshole this time.

Go home, Scottie.

Scottie glanced at her watch. Sorting out her money situation with Tara should be her only concern, anyway, not trying to figure out her boss.

"I'll be back," Scottie said to the group, who had been leaving one by one. Only five remained.

"Where you off to?" Jeff's eyes gleamed at her.

"The ladies room, nosey." Scottie quipped.

He lifted his hands in surrender. "Just making sure you're not bailing on me. Us, I mean."

"My God, Jeff. Do you want to join her in the loo?" Konrad didn't hide his annoyance.

"I'll be back." She'd be back to say goodbye.

In the bathroom, she gazed in the mirror, getting her thoughts together. The pear ale and the scotch may have been a bad mix. She felt a slight lightness, a tingly feeling of intoxication, though not enough to impair her judgement.

When she reemerged from the bathroom and went to the table, only two coworkers remained, Jeff and

Konrad.

Not sitting, she gripped the back of an empty chair. "Where is everyone?"

"They left." Jeff glanced at his watch. "It's nine."

"Already?" It was past her bedtime.

"Time flies when you're having fun," Konrad said, standing to his full, glorious height. He towered over her, as he did everyone.

"I guess so." She pointed to her purse on the table. "Can you please hand me my purse?"

Jeff snatched it before Konrad could. "You're leaving?"

She reached for her purse, tugging harder when he held on playfully. His eyes sparkled, and when he released it, she tucked the purse under her arm. "Yeah. It's getting late."

"Come on. I'll walk you." Konrad moved closer to her. "Close out the tab, Jeff."

Jeff was speechless, and so was Scottie. But, she didn't refuse Konrad. She nodded and said goodbye to a yearning Jeff. His eyes said he wanted to be alone with her, though he dared not defy Lord Korr.

Humidity enveloped Scottie the moment she stepped out of the Bowie Brew. Once they'd exited the bar, she steadily looked down at her pumps with each step and her stomach fluttered all the while. She was alone with Konrad again. He wasn't even a foot from her, and it made her feel anxious. What would he say to her? What would she say to him? Together, they walked, outside of work hours, outside of any formalities. Like they had been at the EaDo property. What would happen at the end of their walk?

For half a block, neither said a word. Each step echoed in her ears, emphasizing the silence between them, though the street had been busy with cars and pedestrians.

"What did you really think of the scotch?" he finally asked, distracting her from counting her steps.

She turned to meet his perfect profile, her lips fighting a smile. "It was awful."

Still looking straight ahead, his lips pulled back, and she swore this man grew even more attractive. "It was atrocious."

She laughed in unison with him and then said, "I guess the Bowie Brew isn't a place to get a good glass of scotch."

He shook his head, wrapping his fingers around her wrist, stopping her from crossing the street. The *no walk* sign had lit up. "That is a correct assessment, *Schatzi*." He looked at her, his mouth still parted from his smile.

Schatzi. The term of endearment he'd called her before.

He had such beautiful lips. She could practically feel them against her mouth.

"What exactly does *Schatzi* mean?" Her voice was husky.

He didn't stall like the last time she'd asked him. "It means sweetheart in German."

She halted her breath until his hand fell from hers. She swallowed. "Oh. That is endearing."

The silence was thick between them again. She didn't know what to say, or how to feel. She was grateful he picked up the conversation where they'd left off.

"You know where to get amazing scotch?" he asked.

"Where?"

"Hugo's."

"I've never been there, but Tara has told me great things about it." She focused on the *do not walk* light.

"You know, Tara, my roommate, the caterer?"

Why am I talking about this? She wanted him to bring up the kiss again.

"Of course. I remember." When the light turned, allowing them to walk, he touched her elbow. She was getting used to him touching her, and it was dangerous.

When they arrived at the parking garage elevator, he pulled her to a halt at the entrance. "What floor are you on?"

"You don't have to walk me all that way to my car." She didn't want him to see her car for some reason she couldn't reconcile. Her car had never been a source of contention for her. It was hers alone, and she was proud of it. But, maybe against Konrad, she felt inadequate. They were from different worlds, though her father's family was wealthy. In fact, it was the money her grandmother had given her for college that allowed her to buy the used car.

He ran a large hand through his dark-gold hair, and her eyes were steady on his fingers—large, strong fingers. "I'm not going to let you walk to your car alone at this time. So I'll ask you again. What floor are you on?"

A thick gulp slid down her throat. "T-the eighth."

He nodded, slipping his hand over her to push a button to summon the elevator. Harder and harder, her heart thumped. Her whole body surged, and she wanted that finger on her. All over her.

The ding of the elevator bell shook her. As the chrome doors slid open, he blocked the track so she could step into the elevator. She didn't know if it was the scotch or him that made her feel woozy, but as she passed inside, she tripped into him, her face smashing against his hard, solid chest. That man was like a brick wall. And he smelled so good.

He moved his palms down her back to stabilize her, though he'd made her feel more wobbly. When she regained her footing, she peered at him, her gaze catching his parted lips. *Oh God...* The apex of her thighs pulsed with all the things he could do to her with those lips. And tongue.

"Watch out. It's a tricky step." His voice was gruff. She was certain he could read her thoughts.

Scottie inhaled, feeling his hard body against her. Straightening, she removed her hands from him, and he dropped his hands from her. Something was going on. Something that started at the EaDo property and hadn't let up.

The bell of the elevator sounded. They'd been blocking the doors too long. Securely inside, he leaned over her and pushed the eighth-floor button.

"I'll tell Susan to give you a VIP parking pass. You'll park on the first floor going forward." It was not a question. It was a command.

"You really don't have to do that." Her voice was so low and lusty she hardly recognized it.

He waved his hand. "It's done."

Both feet on the elevator floor, she knew he would have his way, and she would let him. "Thank you."

The elevator doors opened again, saving her from his magnetism. From his voice. From his body. She needed to get off that elevator or else she'd explode from the emotions bubbling up inside her. She stepped across onto solid ground, though still feeling unsteady. The air in the garage tickled her nose, reminding her where they were.

His steps sounded behind her, and she indulged in wondering if he watched her walk. Watched her hips sway. Could he see how she wanted him? The notion thrilled her. They approached her car quickly, the sedan parked all by its lonesome, popping into plain view at the far end of the empty parking level.

One. Two. Three. She counted to calm herself and fetched her keys. She unlocked the driver's side door and turned to face him. "Thank you for walking me."

In the dim parking garage, his eyes gleamed at her. What was he thinking? The same thing as she had been? He leaned in close, not even three inches from her. She froze. The prospect of him kissing her was real. She braced herself, her whole body sparking with electricity, ready for his lips to take hers again. *Please kiss me.*

He didn't kiss her. Reaching over her, he pulled up the door handle and opened the door. "You're welcome." His voice was gentle, like it had been at the EaDo property.

The tension between them weakened her. Her knees would buckle any moment if she didn't get in her car, but she didn't want to get in just yet. "You know, I think taking this temp job has been the most exciting thing I've done." *And kissing you.*

A curl lifted the side of his lips into a decadent smile, catapulting her desire to new depths. "You've got three more months with me. I hope you can handle all the excitement you have yet to experience."

With me. Yes, everything was clouded by the scotch. She was convinced because she was bolder and more receptive. "I think I can manage."

He licked the corner of his mouth, and God did she want that tongue licking the side of her mouth. She glanced down, her arousal taking her hostage. Still, in that lust-fueled moment, she thought of her wallet. And when she plunged her hand inside her purse, she didn't find it. *Damn.* She'd left it on her desk. What a buzz kill. What they had in the garage would have to end.

"What's wrong?"

"I left my wallet on my desk." Her hand fell from her purse, dangling at her side.

He'd stepped back by then. Yes, their moment was over.

"Come," he said.

In silence, they walked to the office. The tension was palpable. The things unsaid still hung between them. Once they arrived to the suite, Konrad unlocked the door. Scottie glanced at the clock on the wall in the empty reception area. Nine-thirty. Had it only been thirty minutes since they'd left the Bowie Brew?

Konrad emerged from her cube, her wallet in hand. "I found it."

She reached for it, her fingers touching his. The wallet slipped through her fingers, crashing to the floor. Both went for it, their hands touching again. Not just their hands, though. Their faces touched, his lips grazing hers. Shocked, she pulled back, both of them standing and neither grabbing the wallet. Their gazes fused in liquid heat. The air was so dense she could hardly breathe. With equal intensity, they lunged for each other, their lips colliding in a hungry kiss she'd been imagining all day.

Chapter Thirteen

Konrad slipped his tongue in Scottie's mouth. He steam-rolled ahead, taking cues from her body. Nothing could stop him. Not even the prospect of someone lingering in the office after hours could keep him from doing what he'd desired since the moment he saw her.

Cupping her ass, he pulled her hard against his instant erection. Moaning, she ran her palms up his sides to his shoulders. Her lips moved over his, surrendering to him and then taking some control. The woman could kiss, and he savored the mix of scotch and pear on her tongue. God, he wanted to lick every part of her.

Lifting her off the floor, Konrad walked with her into his office, setting her down on his desk. Immediately, she parted her legs, giving him a space to stand over her as they continued their kiss. His hands rode up her smooth thighs. He thanked the gods she decided to wear a skirt that day.

"Konrad?" she asked in a broken whisper.

"Yes?" His lips trailed over her chin and down her throat to her collarbone.

"Should we be doing this?" She slipped her fingers in his trousers' waistband and pulled up his shirt. His stomach rippled at the touch of her fingers on his skin.

"Probably not," he said, unbuttoning her blouse until her white lace bra emerged. He groaned at the perfection of her perky breasts. With little finesse, he pulled a cup to the side and took her nipple in his mouth.

Scottie cried out, her thighs tightening around him. "Maybe we should stop."

He halted all action, his eyes opening. "Do you want me to stop?"

They stared at each other, both of them drawing in sharp breaths. No way did she want him to stop. He could practically smell the need wafting off her body. She bit her bottom lip and tugged his belt loose. No stopping. They would take this to the end.

Scottie pulled Konrad to her, their lips touching again. She licked his lips, coaxing him to open his mouth, which didn't take much. Once he'd opened up, he took control of the kiss. His tongue delved far inside her mouth, exploring every part of her. It was just a precursor to the other places he wanted to put his tongue. He'd show her he was more than capable of giving her the best pleasure she'd ever known.

That was what she had already done for him.

With haste, she slipped off his belt, dropping it to the tiles with a crash. Next came her blouse. She practically ripped it off, tossing it over his chair. She was fiery. Wanton. She knew what she wanted. And it turned him on even more.

As he kissed her, he took off his own shirt and tossed it to the floor. Before he knew it, his trousers were around his ankles, and her skirt was hiked up enough for him to see her panties matched her bra.

"Fuck, Scottie," he groaned, his hands riding up her thighs to touch her. "You're so wet."

She leaned back on her hands, her legs opening wider. "I've wanted you since I kissed you."

"I've wanted you since I first saw you." It was true. He'd desired her before the kiss. Before he'd taken her to the EaDo property. Pulling down the delicate strings of her thong, he slipped her panties down until it dangled from her left ankle. Skin on skin, he settled between her legs. "I hated the way Jeff was flirting with you."

"Were you jealous?" Her tone was bold, brazen.

It was obvious she was aware of the power she had over him.

Before he kissed her again, he growled, "Very."

Konrad would literally do anything for her in that moment. Give her anything.

What an odd feeling for him. He'd thought he was controlling the situation, but he knew now she had all the control.

Their tongues tangled, danced. He couldn't have been any harder, and she couldn't have been any softer. Somehow, in the heat of the moment, he grabbed a condom from his wallet faster than the blink of an eye. In no time he was sheathed and ready to have her—to give her the best orgasm she'd ever had. He gazed down at her, looking for a sign to continue or not.

A seductive look on her face, parted lips, and hooded eyes, gave him the answer he was looking for.

She leaned back. Every part of her was exposed. He groaned at the beauty of her. Scottie took his cock in her hands, stroking him until he thought he might explode. "I want you inside me," she whispered.

No thoughts. Just doing. He entered her, diving through her tight skin. It was so delicious. Her sounds were just as intoxicating as he buried himself inside her. She whimpered until he'd impaled her to the hilt and stopped. His heart pounded. *Fuck.* He could lose it so easily, but he wasn't inclined to do that. Her pleasure was more important than his. He moved back, slowly, watching her face soften with ecstasy with every inch he gave her.

"You're so…" She trailed off.

"What?" he urged.

She bit her lip, her eyes shut tight. "You barely fit inside me."

Konrad knew he had a big cock. It was the one

thing he knew women liked about him. Maybe the only thing. He pressed himself further inside her, hearing her cry out with the depths he conquered. "You can take it."

"I can," she said, pulling him into her again until their lips met in a savage kiss.

Sweat dripped down his back, and when he got too close again, he stopped. This was about Scottie.

"Harder," she begged, digging her fingers into his back.

Harder, he drove insider her. Over and over until her whimpers became moans and her moans became pants. Before he could catch his breath, she clung to him, screaming out his name with her release.

"Fuck, Scottine," he groaned, moving in and out of her over and over until his orgasm came to the surface and exploded in a mass of pleasure he'd not felt in a long time. Never, actually.

Sweaty and shaking from the exertion, they fell limply onto each other.

After a few minutes, or maybe an eternity, Konrad lifted off Scottie, staring at her. *My God. What have I done?*

Chapter Fourteen

Scottie was stone-cold sober. And she felt every conflicting emotion known to man. She stared at Konrad, his face flushed. She was thankful his eyes were downcast. She didn't want to read them. What could they possibly say? When he stood up, not a word out of his mouth, and bent over to lift his boxer briefs over his hips, Scottie knew exactly what he was thinking. She was just another conquest to him. After all, what else could she be?

"Well…" His voice was coarse and disconnected. "This certainly wasn't what I expected."

"Expected?" Her voice cracked. She hated how emotional she sounded.

He looked up, catching her gaze. She became aware of how naked she was.

"Intended." His eyebrows furrowed. The man looked like he was in absolute pain. Not what she expected from a player.

But what did *she* expect? What was *her* intention after their capricious lust had passed? Because it was lust that made her so irresponsible, not just then but also at the EaDo property. She looked down at her fingernails, chipped and in need of a manicure. Not that she ever paid for manicures.

"I didn't intend this either."

She stood, gathering her clothes and reassembling her outfit without looking at Konrad again. She couldn't. The lump in her throat wouldn't let her. *You can walk away from this*. No big deal. Life proved to her men don't stick around. This shouldn't have been so devastating to her. But he'd only been the second man she'd ever been with, and it *was* devastating.

The silence was torture. She wanted him to say something, but at the same time, she didn't. No words were necessary. But all of them were. What did she want? Assurance? Of what? That he wanted her? Or that she was indeed just another notch on his bedpost?

Without looking at him, she walked through his office, Konrad calling her name. She refused to turn and didn't take a single breath. She bent over to retrieve her wallet and her purse, which had fallen to the ground. On the way up, she straightened her spine, shoulders back. *Be strong.* She'd had to learn to be strong where men were concerned her whole life, especially in regards to her heart.

"Scottie, stop," he demanded, his accent strong. She didn't face him. "We should talk about this."

Her eyes closed tight. "I have to go."

"I want to talk about this." His hand warmed her shoulder. She wondered if he'd dressed or if he was still half naked.

Scottie needed to get out of there, needed to be as far away from Konrad as she could. "I-I can't." She dashed out, her shoulder missing his touch on the way out.

Her heart pounded the whole way to her car and to her duplex. Every second of the night replayed in her mind on a loop. Over and over, she tortured herself. She throbbed deep down, still raw from his touch. From his penetration. She whimpered in remembrance.

This is so bad.

Scottie considered staying in her car. She considered driving to her father, though she didn't know where he was, and telling him what she really felt about him. Someone else needed to hear her lament, scream, cry.

Could Konrad be different? No, he couldn't be.

She'd seen the proof. She'd been his accomplice in breaking hearts.

Oh God. She dropped her forehead to the steering wheel.

The whole night could have passed without her moving from the driveway, but the chime of her cell phone brought her to reality. Her stomach tightened. Konrad? She was afraid to check her phone. Too many minutes passed by, and she still didn't answer it. When a hard knock at her window scared the living shit of out her, she jerked her head to the left, her mouth open, her heart blasting inside her chest.

Tara stood, holding her cell phone, a pissed-off look on her face.

Reluctantly, Scottie opened the door and got out to face the music. "Hey."

"Really?" Tara didn't seem to be in the mood.

Scottie ran her fingers through her knotted hair. "I know you're mad."

Tara laughed, not in humor. It might have been what kept her from assaulting Scottie. Her eyes turned up to the dark sky, her sigh long and steady. "You're not giving me a lot of options, Scottie."

Scottie let loose her own long sigh. "I know." She felt like complete shit. This wasn't how she envisioned her life after college. She should be in a career by now, not scrounging to pay rent, putting others in bad positions.

"What am I supposed to do? My catering business is slow-going. I don't have money to support you too, Scott."

"I know." Scottie hated herself more. She needed to do better, say something better than *I know*. "You're right. I can leave." Living in her Nissan for a couple days might be doable. She could go home for a couple of days, though she hated the idea of being in the same apartment with her mom's newest boyfriend.

Tara shook her head. "I don't want to kick you out. I want you to pay me for rent on time every month."

"I know." She should just be quiet. This was so not the time.

"If you can't do that, then we'll have to get another roommate. Brett said he would move in and help with rent."

What? That was the worst thing Scottie could hear. She absolutely couldn't stand Brett. Tara didn't seem exactly excited about that notion, either. It was like a punishment. "No." Scottie's mind reeled, searching for and finding a solution that honestly was a last resort. "I'll pay you tomorrow. I swear."

Her eyebrows lifted. "Tomorrow? You swear?"

"I swear." Scottie shut the door after retrieving her purse. She faced Tara again, who looked curiously at her.

"Where were you? You look weird." Her eyes narrowed. "Have you been crying?"

Scottie froze. Tara always knew when she held back. "I'm just a little bit tipsy. Some coworkers went to the Bowie Brew for happy hour. On the boss's dime." And she was on the boss in his office. *God.*

"Oh."

They walked inside the duplex in silence. With each step, Scottie could feel Konrad inside her. At the doorstep, Scottie turned to Tara, her heart in her throat. "I know I've not been responsible. I'm sorry."

"We all have to grow up, Scottie." Tara's words were harsh, but her voice was soft, and Scottie knew she was right.

She had to grow up. In all aspects.

In her bedroom, Scottie pulled out a box from

under her bed. It had odds and ends she didn't want to get rid of. But what she was looking for was secure in a box, slightly worn from many years. She opened the box, the metal hinges creaking. Inside was an Art Nouveau gold Rene Lalique brooch made for British nurses in 1915. Her paternal grandmother left it to Scottie in her will when she passed away five years ago, along with the college money. The brooch was all she had of her father's family.

And she was going to pawn it.

Chapter Fifteen

The next day, Konrad drove faster to work than usual. Some might even say he drove like a maniac, and he couldn't disagree. He'd become another frustrated Houston driver. He should've been more careful. After all, his car cost six figures.

He couldn't help it, though, and the source of his frustration was not traffic. He should've been more careful about more than just his driving. Scottie had been on his mind since she left him reeling in the office, practically naked. Konrad felt completely exposed emotionally.

It frightened him. What was he supposed to do with the feelings he had?

He eased his sports car into the Korr Corp building parking garage, though his heart didn't let up a bit. He parked up front and center. On his approach, he glanced at the VIP visitor parking spot. Empty. His heart fell. Only two things were feasible. Scottie didn't show up to work. She'd quit, which he half expected but also hated as an option. The other alternative was she'd not parked where he'd instructed her. It was a fifty-fifty. Lifting his foot off the brake after he'd put his car in "park," he breathed in. *Calm the fuck down, Korr*.

With another heavy sigh, he turned off the engine.

Susan had been on a call when he entered the lobby. Waving, he passed her and walked into the suite. He nodded and greeted employees as usual until he turned the corner to his office. And Scottie's cube. His heart came to a complete stop. Images of the night before took him hostage. His tongue in her mouth. His fingers dancing over her skin. Her tight grip around him. Her warmth squeezing his cock. He could have so easily had an erection thinking on it.

He opened his eyes again, taking in the reality of the busy space. Employees moved around him, tasks on their minds. Scottie was on his. When he turned the corner, there she was. In a red dress of all things, which was fitting because he knew she was a no-go. He should have pictured a stop sign the moment he met her. As much as he wanted to rip that red dress off her and put her down on his desk again, his moral navigation system just wouldn't allow it. Apparently, he'd just become aware of the damn system. He hated it. But, he sensed he would hate it more if he ignored it. So would Scottie.

"Hi," he said, his voice too breathless for his taste. He cleared his throat. "Good morning, Scottine." Damn. He didn't know how to act with her anymore.

Her pink glossy lips didn't curl up, didn't give him any indication she was happy to see him. "Good morning, Mr. Korr."

Awkward silence ensued. There was no way she wasn't imagining what they'd done the night before. They'd kissed in the very spot in which they stood. He could see the memory on her face, flushing her cheeks.

"You're looking well." He hoped no other employee could see how Scottie affected him.

Her lip quirked up. "Should I look *un*well?"

His control was MIA, and he didn't know how to proceed. He needed to find it ASAP, though. This was his place of employment, and even though he was an emotional slave to her in that moment, he was still the boss of Korr Corp.

"You didn't park where I told you to." Control came back harsher than he wanted it to. She pursed her lips, and he continued. "Did you forget or just disregarded my instructions?"

"No." She held on to a folder, her knuckles white.

"So why didn't you park where I told you to?"

"I…" She averted her gaze, making him feel bittersweet about his victory. "I—"

"Let's go in my office." So many things to discuss. Urgent things. And none of it was about the stupid parking space.

Scottie made a move toward him, but Jeff's voice put a halt to all their momentum.

"Scottie, there you are." Jeff was too cheery for Konrad's taste, and he had no reason to look for her. Scottie didn't work in his area.

Konrad didn't take his eyes off Scottie, though he clearly needed to vie for her attention from Jeff. *Fuck off.* He was winning, though. Scottie didn't take her eyes off Konrad, either. There was too much unsaid between them.

But when she turned to face Jeff, a smile emerged. The smile Konrad wanted for himself.

"You were looking for me?" She was playful enough to make Konrad's stomach knot up.

This was so fucked.

Jeff beamed, his gaze inching over her face. It was obvious he was interested in her. "I was."

"We're in the middle of something, Jeff," Konrad said, completely aware of his clipped tone. And his jealousy.

Scottie glanced at Konrad. She knew what he was thinking. Her eyes were all-knowing.

"I…" Jeff leaned into Scottie, his voice lower than before, but not low enough. "I wanted to ask if you are free for lunch today. My treat."

It all happened quickly. Scottie met Konrad's eyes again, holding them for a moment.

"You crazy kids should have lunch. But just an

hour, yeah?" Konrad couldn't believe the words came out of his mouth. Scottie looked like she'd been run over by a bus. *You fucking idiot.*

"Sure, that sounds good, Jeff."

Her legs open, him centered between her. His mouth over her nipple, sucking until her moans rolled down his ear. Her sweet smell wafting off her as he buried himself inside her.

No. Fuck no. He couldn't continue this way. Scottie couldn't be just another woman to objectify. She was not like the others.

"Great!" Jeff beamed again and pivoted on his heels, leaving them in painful silence.

Konrad didn't know where to go from there. He must've looked like a complete asshole to Scottie. After they'd had sex not even twelve hours ago, he'd already pushed her in another man's arms. It looked horrible. And, it was not at all what he wanted her to conclude about him. But how could he reconcile his need to be someone different? Someone who wouldn't use women anymore?

"You needed to talk to me in your office?" she asked, her voice huskier than before.

The game to gain his control dissipated. He only wanted to soothe Scottie. "Yes. We need to talk."

He walked into his office, briefcase in hand. Thoughts abounded, though none were clear. Fabian's damn engagement had really screwed up Konrad's flow. He'd been moving along so nicely, but now nothing about what he felt was nice.

Konrad sat, his gaze fixed on Scottie. God, she was so beautiful. Her eyes were downcast. She looked sad, which made him feel like utter shit. He focused on the gold brooch pinned to the right of her V-shaped neckline.

"That's an unusual brooch." He'd zeroed in on it, avoiding what he needed to say.

She looked up at him, her mouth opening as the light bounced off her shiny lips. "It was my great-grandmother's."

He also deciphered a man stretched out, muscles rippling from his back, and wings of a bird sprouting forth. Though it was an interesting pin, it wasn't what he was truly interested in. However, it balanced his focus and slowed the emotions that bubbled under the surface.

"Fascinating." Konrad watched her slim hand reach up to touch the pin. "Heirlooms keep us connected to our family. Our past." Not that he wanted anything from his past. Or family for that matter. His father had proven consistently that family wasn't important. Family was a burden, only necessary for inheritance. He'd certainly inherited the belief for years that marriage hurt and, in his mother's case, was the death of people.

Scottie's eyes glistened. "Yes."

They were silent again. He wished the silence would stop between them. He wished he could say what he felt, that she could say what she felt.

Scottie interrupted his thoughts, the soft voice replaced by indignation. "Why did you tell me to accept lunch with Jeff?"

Could he really tell her the truth? He'd barely been able to tell himself the truth. "Because why not? You need to eat, don't you?"

Her cheeks blazed nearly as red as her dress, and her lips pressed into a straight line. "Because of last night. Here, on your desk. You remember that, don't you?"

He began slowly. Even. Too even, maybe. "Of course I remember last night. I won't forget it. But, it can't happen again. I'm not a guy you want to get involved with. You were right to stop our kiss at EaDo. It was a mistake."

Her fingers tightened over the chair arms, but she didn't say a word.

"I acted unprofessionally. I acted on impulse. And, I admit, I was wrong. I made a mistake. Like you did. Right?" He raked his fingers through his hair. Damn, it was hard to say this to her because he wanted to do it again. He wanted to act on impulse with her. He wanted her to get involved with him. "You're too sweet a girl to want to get involved with a guy like me."

"What about Anisette and Tamsin and Pilar? Are they not too sweet to get involved with a guy like you?" Her voice cracked.

"Scottie..." He hung his head for a moment.

"No." She stood. "You're absolutely right. Last night was a huge mistake. I'm sorry I started it by kissing you. But I know nothing can happen again."

A heavy weight fell on his chest. He wanted to kiss her again. "Can we get past this?"

"Already over it." She turned and strode to the closed door, stopping before she opened it.

"Scottie," he called to her, not wanting her to leave his office that way. She turned back to him, her face solemn. It devastated him. He paused a moment before he could say another word. "You're nothing like Anisette and Tamsin and Pilar."

Her lip trembled, and he thought she might cry. She didn't though. Nodding, she opened the door and walked out without a glance back. He dropped his hands on his desk.

That was not how he wanted the conversation to go. The look on her face made him want to go to her, comfort her. Make her know how he really felt.

A couple of hours later, he walked out to her

cube. He hated the fact that she would have lunch with Jeff. Worse, he hated that he practically forced her to be alone with Jeff. God, if Jeff kissed Scottie, he'd be beyond pissed. The thought made Konrad crazy, and he wanted to cancel their lunch plans.

Scottie turned almost immediately to face Konrad. "Yes?"

"I need you to send a dozen roses."

She didn't hide her eye-roll well. Or her exasperation. "Another?"

"Yes." His stern boss countenance made her straighten. "To Anisette. I want the card to read, 'Congratulations on your engagement.'"

Her eyes grew wide, but she didn't allow her face to betray her further. With a neutral tone, she said, "I will order them immediately. Anything else?"

"That is all."

Another hour later, Konrad was at Hugo's restaurant, glancing down at his watch. He'd worn the Rolex again, not the Richard Mille, which was his favorite. He'd misplaced it.

"Would you care for a drink while you wait on your party?" the waitress asked, taking him from his thoughts.

"Sure. I'll take a scotch, neat." He gazed up and her full lips curled in a smile. Normally, he'd have a thought about them. Have a quick fantasy of what her lips could do to him, but he didn't. He felt nothing.

She waited, her lips straightening out. "I'll be right back."

"Mother fucker, I'll be damned." Dallas approached just as the waitress left. "I worried you wouldn't show up like you didn't last night."

"Keep it down, Halman. This is a classy place, for fuck's sake." Konrad stood, shaking hands with his friend. "You just missed the waitress."

"Damn. Is she hot?" Dallas sat, pushing up his rolled sleeves. The guy hated wearing suits. Konrad knew rancher's dirty jeans and boots were more his style.

Konrad laughed. Typical question. Maybe she was hot, but Konrad was too keyed up to notice. "You can find out for yourself, mate. Here she comes again."

The small brunette waitress arrived with a smile on her face but not Konrad's drink in her hand. "Hello. Would you like to start with a cocktail?"

"Sure, sweetheart." Dallas's east Texas accent grew thicker. Such a move. Konrad rolled his eyes. "I'll have a Gentleman Jack on the rocks."

She nodded, reveling in Dallas's appreciation of her.

Konrad interjected. "Don't be fooled, love. This bloke is not a gentleman at all."

Her cheeks blazed red. "I'll back right back, gentlemen." She winked at Dallas.

They watched her walk away, though it looked like Dallas was enjoying the view way more than Konrad.

"You're such an animal."

A beaming Dallas faced Konrad. "And you're not?" He placed his cell phone on the table next to his sweating glass of water.

Konrad hated that he couldn't disagree. He had been an animal with women for over a decade. A complete dog. He shook his head. Dallas still might be worse. "Not as bad as you, *mien Freund*."

Their eyes met. "I'll take that as a bet."

"Stakes?"

Dallas tossed a paper napkin toward Konrad. "Write down all the names of the women you've hooked up with this month. The one with the most loses. And pays for lunch."

Konrad thought for a moment, counting briefly until the number passed the fingers on one hand. He leaned back, flicking away the napkin. "Nope. A gentleman doesn't kiss and tell."

Dallas threw his head back and laughed. "I'll remember that next time I see one."

Could Konrad really do this? He was compelled to go along with the bet. What was the worst that could happen? He'd either confirm that Dallas was a bigger dog, or he'd face what he'd been avoiding. If he really wanted to turn over a new leaf, he'd have to face it.

"All right, then. I'll take your silly bet." Konrad pulled a Montblanc pen from his jacket pocket. "Prepare to lose."

First, Konrad wrote:
September Hookups
He sighed as the women came forth to his mind. Hell, it was just the beginning of the month. *Shit*. He didn't like this game. Despite the anxiety rippling through him, making him queasy, he continued writing his list.

H Bar Bartendress
Tamsin
Anisette
Hot Yoga Instructor at gym
Pilar
Greek Starbucks Barista on West Gray Ave.
Temp S.R.

His heart stopped. *Bloody hell*. Seven women. He remembered he'd shagged a couple of them on the same day. And two he didn't even remember their names. Guilt and disgust seared through him. And when his gaze came to a stop on Temp S.R., he felt like the worst person in the world. He couldn't even spell out her whole name. Too much shame fell on him. If she knew she was on a running list of hookups, she'd hate him more than she probably already did. Sick to his stomach, he lost his appetite.

"Time's up." Dallas held up his napkin. All entries had names. All *four* of them.

Just then, the waitress arrived with two drinks on her round tray and set them down on the table. "I'll be back to take your orders." She walked away to tend to another table nearby.

"Only four? Dallas, you're slipping." Konrad turned over his napkin. He was too ashamed to look at it anymore. "I concede. I'm the bigger animal."

Dallas grabbed Konrad's napkin, reading with an amused look on his face. "Greek Starbucks Barista on West Gray Ave.?"

Konrad snatched the napkin and shoved it into his suit pocket, along with his pen. "Sod off."

Dallas nearly fell over from laughing, but then he stopped, his eyes narrowing. "Wait. That last one."

Konrad's heart raced. "Yeah?" Nervously, he glanced back to the waitress, signaling for her. He needed an interruption.

"Did it say 'Temp S.R.'?"

Konrad took a hefty gulp. Intoxication needed to come immediately. In the meantime, he refused to acknowledge the question.

"Kon, did you screw your waitress-temp, Scottie?" His voice rose a bit.

Konrad met his demanding gaze. Deny it? Admit it? He didn't know which was smarter. "She's not a waitress."

Dallas's eyebrows lifted. "Did you?"

Dallas was the only one who knew about Scottie, and Konrad needed to unburden himself. "Yes."

Realization came over Dallas. "Last night. You were with Scottie, weren't you?"

"Not exactly. I was at happy hour with my employees like I told you." He took another sip of scotch. The waitress interrupted, for which he was grateful. They each ordered twenty-dollar burgers and resumed the conversation once she'd left. Konrad sighed, feeling more burdened than before he came clean to Dallas, and he didn't want to think of eating anything. "Scottie was at the happy hour. I walked her to her car. And…"

"Dude, please don't tell me you fucked her in the car."

"Fuck off." Konrad felt the heat of anger rise through him. He calmed himself. "No, I did not fuck her in the car. That's so fucking crude, mate."

"Sorry." Dallas lifted his hands in defense.

"She forgot her wallet in the office, and that's where it happened."

"In the office?"

Images of Scottie on his desk, skirt lifted above her hips, panties hanging off her ankle, came to him. He closed his eyes at the remembrance. "On my desk."

Dallas wasn't laughing anymore. He gazed with an intensity that made Konrad refocus on his drink again. He stared into his glass, seeing the night all over again, feeling everything all over again.

"You seem really fucked up about it, Konrad. This isn't like you."

Running his fingers through his hair, he didn't disagree. That was putting it lightly. He was more than fucked up. He was head first in an existential crisis. He was facing his morality. He was facing his belief system and all the things he thought were true about relationships.

He couldn't continue. "Did you see the email about the location for our hotel?"

Dallas frowned. Good thing he knew when to let things go. He was much better at that than Fabian or Tylund. "I did. Are we talking work now?"

"We are." Konrad noticed his phone blink with a message. He picked it up, reading Fabian's text. A brunch-on-the-yacht invitation for Sunday. "Pallis is having a thing on the yacht this weekend."

"Oh, right. He mentioned that last night. You going?"

"I don't see why not." The sun and wind would do him good. Clear his mind. Make him see there was a world outside of his. "It should be right fun, yeah."

"It always is on Pallis's yacht."

"Is he catering?" Konrad couldn't help the question. Would he see Scottie again outside of the office?

"I think he mentioned that same girl who catered the other night." Dallas stopped mid-drink, his eyes meeting Konrad's. "Oh shit. Do you think Scottie will be working?"

Konrad's pulse quickened. He needed Scottie to be on the yacht. "I don't know."

The waitress arrived with their meals. Several bites into his lunch, Konrad still couldn't get Scottie out of his mind. "I know I should not have shagged my temp. It was fucking moronic. I was too attracted to her because of the way she judged me, I think, which is so demented when you think about it."

He didn't dare look up to Dallas, whose full attention he knew he had and who didn't tussle him about his inarticulate thoughts. "But immediately afterward," he went on, "I felt like she wasn't just another hookup. She wasn't just another fling I'd forget about. But I'm just like my father, right? I can't see myself having these thoughts, but I do."

The silence stretched between them despite the noise in the restaurant. Dallas finally said, "You're not your father, Kon."

Konrad looked up to his friend, their eyes meeting and holding for several beats until the waitress interrupted them again.

"How is everything?"

"Fantastic, darlin'," Dallas said, winking at her.

Konrad only nodded his approval. Everything was far from fantastic, but perhaps if he could accept he wasn't noncommittal like his father, it could get better.

Chapter Sixteen

Scottie could not stop thinking about Anisette. She'd gotten engaged? Did that mean Konrad had lost a woman? Needed a replacement? Oh God, she would not be that replacement!

Even knowing the reality of the situation, why did she still want him?

"Are you okay?"

"Uhh … yes." She glanced at Jeff, offering a forced smile. They'd taken a later lunch than expected. La Carotte, a small French restaurant, was in walking distance of the office.

"This is beautiful!" She scanned the tiny space. Only twelve tables lined the walls facing outside the massive windows onto the street on all four sides.

"I got us a reservation earlier. I hope we can still get a seat since we're an hour late." He pressed his hand on her lower back.

Her first instinct was to jump away from his touch, but the approaching host made it impossible.

"*Bienvenue. Bonne après-midi.*" The host, an older man wearing faded black jeans and a long-sleeved gray shirt, greeted them. He had a modern haircut, short on the sides, long on top and a graying beard.

"*Bonjour*, Etienne," Jeff said with a bad accent.

"Ahh, you've brought a date this time." Etienne winked, patting him on the arm.

Jeff laughed. "This is Scottie."

Etienne bowed his head. "Pleasure."

"I'm his coworker," Scottie said, refusing to look at Jeff. She didn't like the insinuation. They were *not* on a date. "This is such a beautiful restaurant."

"Wait until you taste the food," Jeff said from

behind her.

"This guy is too much, *mademoiselle*." Etienne laughed. "Follow me."

Agreed. It was all too much. Had Konrad not forced her to accept, she'd be at her desk eating a sandwich from one of the first-floor kiosks.

At their corner table, Scottie sipped her iced water and stared out of the window. Images of Konrad infiltrated her mind. His touch. His smell. His mouth. If only Jeff could read her thoughts, he wouldn't have asked her to this fancy French lunch.

"How do you like working for Konrad?" Jeff's voice pulled her out of her reverie.

Not a single word came forth. How did she like working for Konrad? She wasn't sure anymore. "It's fine."

"Really?" His dark eyebrows lifted.

She shrugged. *Play it cool.* "I mean, the work is whatever. Copying, setting appointments—" Having sex on his desk. *Oh God.*

"Sending flowers to his women." Jeff laughed.

A wave of energy spiked through her. She didn't like that. "Doing personal errands for him."

"So how many women does he have? I heard seven regular women." He sipped from his glass Coke bottle, leaving the empty glass filled with ice the waitress brought to sweat.

Seven regular women? When was that? She sighed. This should be more evidence that it was a mistake to hook up with him. It was over. No harm, no foul. Why was that so hard to believe?

"I don't know. I don't ask questions." Scottie rubbed the cold water drops running down her glass. "I'm just a temp."

He leaned back in his chair. "I gotcha. I guess it's

best to stay professional with him."

Too late. How was Scottie supposed to enjoy the rest of lunch?

"How does he feel about employees dating?" She didn't look at him when she posed the question.

"It's against policy."

Scottie looked up to Jeff, his eyes sparkling. "Well, I guess I'm not going to date anyone at Korr Corp." She had no idea why she asked him that question. It only seemed to fuel some fire Jeff had been building since she met him on the grand tour of Korr Solutions.

Without missing a beat, Jeff said, "You're not a Korr Corp employee, though."

No, she most certainly was not. She also was most certainly done with the conversation.

After the awkward lunch, Scottie returned to the office only when she'd made a detour to Space City Pawn, without Jeff. She counted the twelve hundred dollars she got for the pin, which was an insult. She should have gotten three times that much for it, but beggars couldn't be choosers. She swore she'd never be a beggar again. She couriered her portion of the rent in cash to Tara. What was done was done.

Konrad came back to the office around three, holding a small bag with handles. He stood in her cube, commanding her complete attention, which wasn't hard to give. Every nerve ending sparked at the sight of him. Distressed jeans, chambray button-up shirt with the sleeves rolled to the elbows and Converse sneakers. Sunglasses were perched on top of his head, and his bergamot scent made her quiver deep inside. She liked his casual style as much as she liked him in a suit.

"I need you in my office for the rest of the afternoon." He pointed in the direction of his office. "We need to work on a major presentation for Monday afternoon."

Scottie stood, promptly grabbing a notepad and purple ink pen, trying to hide the exhilaration that ran through her. "No problem."

Denying her continued attraction to him was impossible.

Stoic, and with no indication he shared her thoughts, he simply said, "Come."

Come. The one word sounded obscene from his lips, and it made her remember everything he'd done to her. On that same desk were the residual images of them succumbing to desire—the desire that was clearly still there for her, despite the fact he'd called it a mistake that morning. She'd agreed with him. Correction, her brain had. Her body had come to a different conclusion.

Scottie followed Konrad into his office. How was she supposed to act around him? *Let him lead.* The only person she could control was herself.

Konrad met her at the round conference table at the far end of his vast office. "How was your lunch?"

The words sounded nonchalant, but the clench in his jaw suggested he was jealous. Was he jealous like he'd been last night on his desk, when they...

Stop it.

"It was fine." With her fingertips, she skimmed the pile of folders he'd set down.

"Glad to hear it. I hope Jeff was a gentleman." The folders had his attention as he said the words.

"He was."

Then he lifted his eyes to her, pinning her gaze. "Good. I'll fire him if he wasn't."

The breath hitched in her throat. *Oh God.* That stare. Eyes shifting down, she busied herself with the folders. "What's this meeting for?"

"Ortho-Sync, the medical device manufacturing

company, is interested in making a bid for the EaDo property." He pulled out two chairs next to each other. "I want them to buy the property."

Scottie's gaze danced over his fingers, which were curled over the backs of the slate-gray ergonomic chairs. Those fingers... "Okay."

Two hours later at five o'clock, when the other employees were calling it a day, Scottie continued to type on Konrad's laptop as he spoke. She'd created the presentation live, feeding off his energy. But one thing came to mind. "This is the same property that Bayou Sling Brewery bid on."

He'd run his fingers through his hair multiple times by that point. "Correct. But they can't compete with Ortho-Sync. They don't have enough investors to pull in the two million. Close, but not close enough."

Scottie glanced back at the computer screen in quiet contemplation. "You won't consider it?"

Suddenly, Konrad moved across the room fast and opened a drawer in his desk to rummage through it. Then he emptied out all three drawers and reassembled them again. "God, I thought I remembered where I'd left my Richard Mille watch. But no ... I guess not."

"You lost it?"

His hand gripped the back of his neck. "I have no idea where I left it." He walked back to the round table. "It's such a sad shame because it's my favorite watch."

"I'll keep an eye out for it."

His lips slightly curled up in a smile. "Thank you." As he sat next to her again, the skin on his arm touched hers, singeing her, but she didn't pull away.

What were they talking about? With Konrad so close to her, she couldn't focus. All she wanted to do was lean in, kiss him as she had when they were last alone in his office. When he'd had her naked.

Konrad cleared his throat, startling her from her reverie. "No, I can't."

Scottie averted her gaze to the laptop keyboard, her mind on their conversation they'd had in the morning. Had he read her mind? Embarrassed, she said in haste, "Yeah, I know you can't. You don't have to say it again"

The moment he touched her wrist, she stopped typing. "What do you mean, again? I know for a fact the property can get much more. So no, I can't consider it."

Warming with even more embarrassment, she remembered her question about Bayou Sling Brewery. *I'm such an idiot.*

"Oh. Sorry. I was thinking of something else. Sorry." Changing the subject, she continued, "Will you let them try to outbid Ortho-Sync if they can get more investors?"

"Of course. This is business after all. But I know they've tapped out and won't get the capital."

Scottie looked him square in the eyes when she'd contained herself. "Maybe you shouldn't underestimate them." She might have been thinking about herself, and not just the Bayou Sling Brewery.

Chapter Seventeen

Konrad glanced outside the window. Dark sky and downtown lights streamed through his office. It was nearly nine in the evening. Long day indeed. Scottie typed away, the clicks grating on his nerves. How had he managed to keep his hands off her when she'd been not even a foot from him for hours on end?

He gazed at her, her lips bare and her hair tucked behind her ears. He imagined for hours what her bra looked like under her red dress. Lace. Mesh. Satin. He liked it all, but he'd like it more if she didn't have on a bra. Or panties either.

Aroused again, he needed to stop thinking about her in such terms. She was not an object for him to lust over. Dear God, he wanted to objectify her, though. But in a good way, if that was possible.

"I think this calls for a drink, yeah?" Konrad stood, walking to his desk. He'd bought a bottle of scotch from Hugo's after he'd had lunch with Dallas. The one he'd told Scottie about.

"Sure." The keyboard clicks followed that single word.

Excitement rushed through him. Taking two glasses from his bar on the way back to the table, he said, "I have a surprise for you."

Head tilted, eyes narrowed, she asked, "You do?"

"I do." Once he'd returned, he placed the glasses on the table, the satin bag still in the other hand. "Remember when I told you Hugo's has the best scotch?"

"Yes." Her eyes focused on the satin bag he'd opened.

"I present to you..." Konrad slipped out the

smooth, thick square glass bottle. "…Mortlach twenty-five year. It is my absolute favorite."

Her eyes widened. "That's the twenty-five year?"

"It better be the twenty-five year!" He laughed, setting the bottle next to the glasses.

"That must have been expensive."

He shrugged. "Some things are worth the price tag." He'd paid a much heftier price for the bottle since it wasn't from the auction where he normally bought all his scotch and wine.

She took the glass Konrad handed her, her face slack in contemplation. "You like buying things for people, don't you?"

True, he did spend a good amount of money on friends and non-friends alike. It was how he expressed himself, good or bad. It was how his father expressed himself as well. Money and things always pleased people. Positive reinforcement was what his father had called it.

"It's always a crowd-pleaser."

He poured the amber liquid in Scottie's glass until it was an inch high.

"Is that what you want? To please the crowd?" She lifted the glass to her nose and sniffed.

He poured more than an inch in his glass. "Don't you like being pleased?"

Their eyes met. Nothing could be heard except their breathing.

"Is that a real question?" Scottie's voice was a near whisper.

Konrad had affected her. He could see it in her darkened eyes, her quivering lips. How he wanted to take that lip between his teeth and tug until she moaned.

"Tell me. Does this scotch please you?" Dangerous ground. He should not have asked that question. It wouldn't lead him anywhere safe, but he didn't want to play it safe. He wanted to go on impulse, not reason. Hadn't he learned his lesson? Clearly, not.

Her eyelids fluttered down to the glass. She hesitated before sipping the liquid, her cheeks flushed pink. It was getting a bit hot in the office. Everyone had left by then, and the air-conditioning had been turned up to seventy-five degrees by default.

He waited, watching her lips press together. A tiny curve formed on her lips, and he knew she was pleased. No words necessary.

"Yes." She placed the glass on the table. "This is the best I've ever had."

The best I've ever had. She might have been talking about his cock and not the scotch by the way she looked at him. His lust was off the charts, and he wanted to be the best she'd ever had in bed. He wanted to be the best kisser she'd ever had. He wanted to have the biggest cock she'd ever had. He wanted to go down on her and give her the best orgasm she'd ever had.

He looked away, placing the glass on the table as well. *Get it together, Korr.* What had they just talked about that morning? But his desire for her was too strong at that point. It was a growing force that could take over at any second.

"Konrad?" She appeared concerned and drew closer to him. Her high heels tapped lightly against the tiles. "Are you okay?"

"No." He was surprised by his answer.

Her warm fingers wrapped around his bicep. "Why?"

He met her wide eyes, taking in her beautiful face centimeter by centimeter. The makeup had worn off and she was more beautiful than ever. "You have no idea what you do to me, Scottine. No idea how much I've had to control myself being so close. I have no idea how my goddamn penis hasn't torn through my trousers the whole time we've been in here."

She gasped, removing her fingers from him. "But you said—"

He scrubbed his hair with one hand. "I know what I said. And I still say it."

"And I still agree," she quickly added.

But he didn't *still* say it. And he knew she didn't *still* agree.

"It's late," he said. "We should call all this to a halt and start up early on Monday morning."

"O-okay." Her footsteps sounded again as she gathered her things from the round table.

Konrad walked over to his desk, a gargantuan sigh escaping him. His emotions roiled inside him. He'd need to drink the whole bottle of Mortlach once she left.

"I'm leaving now." Scottie approached him minutes later, her hands full and her face empty.

"Good night, then. Have a nice weekend." The ache inside him grew.

She nodded and a slow-motion pivot followed as she went for the door.

Konrad never disregarded his decisions concerning women, but the urge to have her moved him to defy himself. He reached for her wrist before she turned away from him. Her arms flailed, dropping folders to the floor.

Without a word, he pulled her into him, their eyes fusing. Before he knew it, their lips slammed into a violent kiss that forced them both to their knees

Chapter Eighteen

Scottie let Konrad kiss her. She wanted it just as much as he did, despite what they'd said. It felt too good to deny him.

His hands explored her back and her ass with the expertise she'd experienced before. Before they could go further down the lust hole, he pushed her away, startling her.

Breathless, he said, "Well, I obviously can't control myself."

"Obviously." Scottie held her breath, her mind reeling.

"I should fire myself." There was an uncertainly in his voice that she'd never heard before. He seemed completely perplexed, unhinged.

"I agree." Could they just be normal again? Like they were when she first walked into Korr Properties?

He trailed his fingertips up her arm until he reached her throat, his thumb settling in the dip at her throat. "I don't know what to do from here."

Scottie's heart raced. *Oh God.* She didn't know either.

He lifted his head, his gaze meeting hers, his hand dropping. "We are attracted to each other. That's more than obvious."

She didn't say a word. Everything was getting complicated. He was too tender in that moment, and she wanted him to be an asshole. Fire her, maybe. Something to make her not like him, not want him anymore.

"You're not my type." Scottie pressed her lips together, though her heart soared at the way his eyes gleamed at her. "I'm not into players."

"And you shouldn't be."

What the hell was this conversation? He should have left her alone. They needed to leave each other alone. End of story.

"Can I buy you dinner?"

Seriously? Had he just asked her on a date?

"Okay," she said, going against her inner voice. So much for leaving each other alone.

Thirty minutes later, at almost ten at night, they snagged a table at Uchi, a trendy sushi place in lower Montrose. Yet another place she'd never been to. Did he always take his women to posh restaurants? Not that she was his woman. Or his anything.

Scottie was glad she'd worn her best fitted dress to work that day. At least she was dressed for the restaurant.

"Have you been here?" Konrad brushed a rogue wave from her forehead, her whole body tingling at his touch.

She glanced to the side because his action felt too intimate for a public place. She didn't expect him to touch her at all in front of people. "No, I haven't."

"But you like sushi, yeah?"

Nodding, Scottie looked at the approaching hostess who gazed at Konrad. No question the hostess liked what she saw. Every woman in the restaurant did. Konrad was one of those men who made heads turn, made married women question their fidelity.

"This way, *Mr. Korr*." His name sounded odd on the hostess's lips. Insinuating as if she knew him, or knew of him.

They followed her to the corner of the restaurant near the end of the bar. It was the most secluded part of the restaurant. Scottie sat with her back to everyone. Her focus was Konrad.

"It's quiet back here." She set down her purse

next to her on the wooden bench of the intimate booth for two.

"Like it's just the two of us in the whole world." He winked at her.

Her stomach fluttered. Why did he have to torture her? Would she survive this dinner? This whole damn thing?

"We would probably tire of each other if that was true." She took one of the two menus the hostess had left on the table.

He laughed. "You would probably tire of me first."

She gazed at his beautiful face. *Impossible.* "Probably."

Another laugh fell from his lips, the lips she couldn't stop looking at. The ones that kissed her in a way that no one else had. He looked up from the menu to meet her eyes. "You wouldn't be the first."

Scottie hated that statement. No, she wasn't his first anything. She understood what he was. "Do you pick women who would tire of you?"

He leaned back. "What kind of question is that?"

Scottie shrugged. "I'm curious."

"Didn't curiosity kill that cat?" A smirk lifted the side of his mouth. Clearly, he didn't want to have a serious conversation, not about his choice in women at least.

Maybe that was for the best. She didn't really want to know about him and other women. She'd had her fill of it already.

She shook her head, not knowing where to go from there. Distracting herself from the issue of their attraction to each other, she scanned the menu, deciding on a sake cocktail. Alcohol might not be a good idea, but she needed some kind of liquid courage to continue in the casual way he insisted upon. She could not be casual, and she worried what that would mean for her gainful temporary employment. But even more, what would it mean for her heart?

"Scottie," he said, his deep voice thrumming through her ears. Her gaze zeroed in on his partially opened mouth. Though the act was quick, Scottie imagined he swiped his tongue along his bottom lip in slow motion. He continued to speak. "I like you."

"Oh…"

"I've never done this with an employee."

"I'm not your employee." She said it to remind herself, but what difference would that make?

"Fine. With someone who works with me."

She averted her eyes to the menu again. Why did he have to look at her like that? Like he was being honest, and not running a line.

"Scottie?"

She met his gaze.

"I want you to know that. You are the only one." Blue eyes glittered from the candlelight flickering in the center of the table.

The waitress interrupted them at the perfect time. Scottie was at a loss for words. Konrad had been too gentle. Her feelings mattered to him. She could see it plain as day.

But then what? How would they stop the attraction between them? Because it was there more than before. She felt it in her bones, like a vibration inside her.

"Have you decided on a cocktail? Maybe a glass of sake or wine?" The waitress kept a steady gaze on Konrad.

Does she know him?

Konrad looked at Scottie, moving his hand across the table to touch hers. "Would you like to get a bottle of sake?"

Warmth of his touch spread through her fingers. "Uh … sure. Okay."

He smiled, his gaze moving back to the waitress, who frowned then. "We'll take the premium *Ginjo* sake. Chilled."

"Of course." The waitress turned away, her topknot swaying with her sharp departure.

Konrad watched the waitress leave, his gaze on her back. Not gawking or obscene.

"She likes you." Scottie pulled his eyes to her.

Chuckling, he said, "I'm sure she likes everyone in her table section."

"She must really like this table."

Konrad looked her square in the eyes. "You're jealous."

Heat crawled up her body. "Not at all. I've been on that ride."

His eyebrows raised. "And it was the best ride you've ever been on. I was there, remember? I heard the panting."

Her cheeks burned with embarrassment and remembrance. Konrad was crass enough to go there. She should've remembered it when she wanted to push his buttons. But he was right. It was the best ride she'd ever been on, and she wanted to get on again.

Scottie averted her gaze. "You'll never know for sure."

"Perhaps." He said it as if they weren't over, as if their tryst was to be continued despite what they'd agreed on.

"Perhaps?" She couldn't let it go.

Their eyes met again. All the lust that was between them drew them in. She was paralyzed with his magnetic eyes. His pull. Her desire to have him again.

Regret would come either way if she went along with her feelings.

Plump lips curled up at her, beckoning her. "Perhaps."

They were not over. Nothing was more evident. They were, in fact, still very much *on*.

"Should we even be here?" Scottie was breathless. "I don't know what we're doing here, Konrad."

"Having a meal. We have to eat, don't we?" His lips rested together with such ease that she felt even more uneasy.

"You know that's not what I mean." Maybe she should just shut up and enjoy it. She did have fun with him when they were like this, playing and teasing each other. But her heart might make it something it wasn't. Obviously, it already had.

Konrad reached over the small table, setting his hand over hers in one of the endless ways he insisted on touching her. "Can't you just enjoy dinner with me?"

"How?" She lifted her thumb, moving it over the smooth skin of his forefinger. She had to touch him back.

The silence took her. Nothing penetrated the wall they'd built around them in that small corner booth.

He chuckled low. "I don't know. Just eat and drink and enjoy it." He slid his hand up her wrist and over her forearm. His palm dwarfed her. She felt absolutely tiny against him.

"It's hard to think about enjoying a meal when you're touching me like this." Their point of contact became her focus. His pulse quickened against her skin.

He removed his hand, abandoning her. She missed it immediately.

"I won't touch you, then, if you don't enjoy it." His eyes darkened.

"We decided this was a bad idea."

The waitress arrived with a bottle of chilled sake and two small porcelain cups. Her interruption couldn't have been more poorly timed.

Scottie didn't take her eyes off Konrad. He didn't take his eyes off her either.

"Are you ready to order? Or do you need more time?"

"More time," Scottie snipped, surprised at her response.

The waitress furrowed her brow, her face betraying her required calmness. "Of course. Take your time." She left the table yet again in a jerk. Scottie was sure the waitress hated them, or more accurately her.

Konrad tilted his head. "Do you know what you want?"

What a question. Was he talking about dinner in general or, specifically, the situation they'd found themselves in?

"Do you?" she challenged him, despite her better judgement. The electricity between them was on high power.

He laughed. "Answering a question with a question."

She smiled slow, feeling a high with the way he looked at her mouth. "Yes."

He grew serious then, leaning in. "I always know what I want, Scottine." His voice was low, seductive. And she was falling for it. Again.

Desire took her captive. Fuck what they'd said. She wanted Konrad, and she didn't care what the consequences were. Their attraction had been off the charts, something she'd never experienced before. Or allowed herself to experience. But there it was, in her face, taking her hostage.

The waitress came over again, startling Scottie, though Konrad seemed unaffected. "Have you decided?"

With ease and a coolness that Scottie could not have pulled off, Konrad said, "We'll be ordering to go."

Chapter Nineteen

It all happened so fast. Lightning fast. Konrad had his head between Scottie's legs, kissing her skin, moving with the lust that he'd harbored for days. He pushed her panties harder to the side, licking her until she'd squeezed her thighs against his face.

"God, you're so good." She opened her legs and shoved her hands raking through his hair. Breathless, she said, "I had no idea it could be like that."

Moving up her body, he nipped her skin until his lips touched hers. He wanted her to know how good she tasted. Their tongues touched, danced.

They were on his California king bed in his penthouse. He couldn't recall how they got there. All he remembered was speed and hands and lips and his cock so hard he'd thought it would burst. And Scottie in his bed—the first to ever be in his bed.

His decision-making malfunctioned in regards to her. He wanted to give her the best pleasure she'd ever known, that was a given. But he wanted more, especially after having her in his bed. But he wasn't sure how to progress past the physical. He'd never given or received more than that. How would he do it? Would he be successful at the aspects of a normal relationship? He was wading through unchartered waters without a life jacket.

Scottie wrapped her legs around his waist. Warm and soft, her skin was his comfort. He pressed her against the bed with his weight. She jammed her hand between their hot, writhing bodies, pulling up her dress over her hips. His palms formed over the tops of her thighs, the urgency to be inside her taking over.

"Scottie…" He choked on his words. "I want you

so fucking bad."

"I want you too. Please…"

Konrad groaned, wanting to hear her beg for him. He tore off his chambray shirt, the buttons crashing against the tiles. Just as fast, he unbuckled his belt, pushing down his jeans to expose his thick erection. She gasped in response to him, and he couldn't be more pleased.

"Let me get a condom," he grumbled, though it didn't take away from their momentum. He tore through his wallet, pulling a square packet from its depths. When he was properly sheathed, he slipped his hands under her ass and lifted her to him, his tip at her entrance.

"Oh God," Scottie yelped, lifting her pelvis to receive him. And with a slight move, he slipped inside her.

The tension appeared to have rendered her speechless. She was so small. She'd feel the entirety of him when he was done with her. Leaning in, he kissed her neck, soothing her cries as he buried himself inside her.

"You feel so good," he whispered against her throat.

She wrapped her arms around him. Their naked flesh sealed together with the beading perspiration from their slick bodies moving together.

"Oh Konrad," Scottie whimpered, her legs tightening around him.

Heat circulated inside him, concentrating at center. She turned her face, groaning for him, begging him to go faster. The threat of orgasm came fast, but he didn't want to release yet. Slowly, he moved his hips to maintain a rhythm that kept him on the edge. She, on the other hand, clenched around him, her orgasm coming forth. He could feel it with every move and every sound she made.

"Are you close?" he asked, his lips pressing against her jaw.

Without a response, Scottie cried out again with his movements. He'd grown harder, thicker, and he wasn't having any mercy on her.

"Faster," she urged, the word getting caught in her throat.

He complied. Grabbing her ass again, he lifted up her hips, slamming into her as if his heartbeat depended on it. Faster and faster, he impaled her, eliciting cries and moans and pleas to not stop.

"Konrad!" she cried in ecstasy.

Konrad closed his eyes, driving inside her, his orgasm forming stronger than before. He grunted, his fingers digging into her buttocks. His lips fell on hers with his final grunt, kissing her like a starved animal. He dove his tongue in her mouth, tasting her, teasing her. Owning her.

It was the most pleasurable thing he'd ever felt.

"I think I could be here with you like this for a very long time." The words came out, unfiltered, unconsidered. The longer she didn't respond, the harder his heart knocked against his chest.

They were silent for a while. His breath slowed, as did his heart. He wanted to be there with her. He wanted to share his bed with her, and he felt no anxiety about her presence in his home. Before, his home had been off limits. He'd had a select few over, but not one woman touched his bed or spent the night.

Konrad wasn't sure how long they'd stayed in the bed when the doorbell rang several times. His body surged up, lifting from their warm embrace, and he turned to face his phone sitting on the side table. It blinked with text messages. *Who in bloody hell could that be?*

Scottie sat up, holding the sheet against her naked body. "Are you expecting someone?"

It was the hostess, Jenny, from Uchi. How did she know where he lived? They'd had a dalliance earlier in the year when he'd first arrived to Houston, but he hadn't seen her since then. He should have acknowledged her at Uchi the moment he walked in, but how would that have looked in front of Scottie? She'd be even more convinced he was an asshole. A player.

"No, I'm not," he said in reply to Scottie's question and swung his legs over the bed, picking up his phone. "But, I'm about to have terse words with the concierge."

A number he didn't recognize had texted him hours ago when he was at Uchi. He must have deleted Jenny's number when he'd deleted her from his rotation.

He'd missed a couple of texts from earlier in the evening when he'd arrived at the restaurant.

Unknown: **Are you seriously acting like you don't know me?**

Unknown: **Is she one of your women? Does she know how many you have?**

The last text message had been minutes ago when the doorbell rang. This was his worst nightmare.

Unknown: **Can we talk? Are you home?**

Furious, he moved his fingers over the keyboard.

Me: **I don't know how you found out where I live, but if you don't leave immediately, I'll call the authorities.**

Cell phone in hand, he stormed through his bedroom, down the corridor, and through the long living room until he reached the door. Peering through the peephole, he didn't see anyone. His heart calmed, but he was still furious. How could he be so reckless? This wasn't what he wanted. It especially wasn't what he wanted Scottie to see.

"Was that one of your women?" Scottie's voice came from behind.

He closed his eyes, his heart falling. *Fuck*. He turned, meeting her hardened gaze. How could he answer her?

"Will I have to send another bouquet of flowers on Monday?" Her words crushed him.

I'm such an asshole.

"It's not what you think." It was absolutely what she thought. And more. He scrubbed his face. "She's someone I had a fling with earlier this year. That's all. I haven't seen her since."

Scottie crossed her arms over her chest, spinning on her heels back through the living room with him following behind her until they reached the bedroom again.

"I don't know who you are, Konrad." She collected her clothes. "I see the Konrad who I swear makes me feel like I am the only person in the world, and then I see the other Konrad who has a different woman every day. Women who show up at his house unannounced. Women I have to send flowers to."

He reached for her, though she pushed his hands away. He let out a sound of frustration. "You *are* the only person in the world right now."

"Right now." Her anger flashed through her ever-changing eyes.

"That's not what I meant." *Dammit*. He kept screwing up, saying the wrong thing. This was not his game. He had no idea how to get her back to where she was before the doorbell rang, when they'd been comforting each other, and he was thinking how much he liked her in his bed.

In a flash, she was dressing and walking across the massive bedroom again.

"Wait, Scottie." He followed her, completely naked and not giving a shit. "Don't leave. Talk to me. Please."

She turned, her face flushed. "I can't help how attracted I am to you, Konrad."

"And I can't help how much I am attracted to you." The sweet feel of relief was on the wings, waiting to return. He needed to know she'd still want him when he could do this better, when he knew how to treat her the way she deserved.

"But I also know what I get with you." She waved her hands in exasperation. "I can't do this. Every time I think about who we are, I know this is too much for me. It affects me in a way you don't understand."

"Then tell me," he pleaded, which sounded so odd. He'd never seen this side of himself. "I want to understand."

Her teeth worried over her bottom lip and for a brief moment, he thought she was going to tell him. Instead, she shook her head. "I can't fall for someone like you. I'll hate myself."

She turned, dashing from his room and through the living room and in the direction of the exit.

"Wait. Let me at least drive you back to the office if you're not going to stay." She'd left her car there.

"No. I'll order a car." She bumped her leg on the white leather sectional on the way to the door. He followed her, his wide stride keeping up with her fast legs with no problem.

"Be careful, love. Don't hurt yourself."

Spinning around just before she reached the front door, she held her hands up, making contact with this chest. "Stop it! Stop being sweet, Konrad. That makes it harder to not like you, to not want you."

"You don't have to go. You don't have to make a decision about me this very moment."

Their eyes met, lingered. Would she stay? He had no idea. He knew absolutely nothing about what she would do or say.

"I work for you."

"You work for A-Plus Temporaries." The need to take her in his arms was intense, but he didn't dare touch her, not after she dropped her hands from his chest.

"Yes, you've mentioned it."

"I don't feel the same as before." Words flew from his mouth, words he should have kept inside. "I don't want to be who you think I am."

"But you are." Her voice was soft.

When she turned, he felt the biggest hole in his chest emerge. Complete emptiness inside. And just like that, she was on the other side of the door. His forehead fell against it after it closed.

In a whisper, he said, "You'll see. I'm not."

****

In the morning, Konrad opened his eyes, despite the brutal sun slicing in through the opened blinds in his bedroom. He reached for his phone, checking for Scottie's response to the text he'd sent her after she'd left him.

Me: **Please let me know you're safe.**

Nothing. She'd not responded. She might regret giving him her number, because he intended to contact her whether she wanted him to or not. He put his fingers on the screen, typing another message, then rereading it twice but not pressing send.

Instead, he deleted his overly emotional message. God, this was not like him. And, fucking hell, it was such torture to feel the way he did—out of control, desperate, needy, yearning. It all sucked.

He typed a message to Dallas instead.

Me: **I need a cocktail. Brunch?**

He glanced at the clock. It was after ten in the morning. He normally didn't sleep that late. Usually, he'd been to the gym by then.

Dallas: **I'm down. Mariposa? I need to talk hotel stuff with you.**

Me: **An hour.**

Dallas: **Cool.**

An hour later, Konrad sat at the Halman Hotel bar. Dallas had already arrived and was typing on his computer into a maps and navigation application.

"Running comps?" Konrad sat next to him at the bar where they'd met so many times before. He nodded to the bartender, Bea.

"Bloody Mary?" she asked from across the bar.

"Yes, love." Konrad slapped Dallas on the back. He'd hoped the short drive to the Museum District would calm him. It had done the opposite. He wanted to expel everything that happened. "How's it going, mate?"

"Not bad, my friend." Dallas looked up from the laptop, the sun rays catching his brown eyes. "I think I got us a better location. It's not on the market yet. I got a tip."

"Tips are good."

"Indeed." Dallas turned his laptop toward Konrad. "You know the Le Petite Moreau?"

"Of course. It's a world-renowned posh boutique hotel. Why?"

The Bloody Marys arrived, set on thick monogramed coasters. Dallas lifted his glass to Bea. "Thanks, sweetheart."

"My pleasure. I'll come back to take your orders." She walked away to tend to other patrons.

"Well…" Dallas pointed to the location on the map. It was perfectly tucked away in the heart of the Montrose neighborhoods. "Moreau is getting out of the hotel business."

"No shit!" Konrad was stunned. "How do you know this?"

Dallas closed the laptop with emphasis. "I talked to Moreau myself."

"How in bloody hell did you snag an appointment with Jacob?"

A crooked smile emerged from his lips. "I didn't. I ran into him yesterday while I was in Dallas last night checking on the Dallas Halman location. He just happened to be in the bar having a drink after dinner."

"So, you just shot the shit with the lad? Like no big deal?" If Konrad had a man crush, it was for Jacob Moreau, mogul extraordinaire. The man made more money in a day than Konrad made in a year. Konrad's eight figures a year was mere pocket change to Jacob Moreau.

"It was casual as fuck, but we got to talking, and he's decided to sell his hotel and concentrate on pharma and technology."

"My God, the man has his hands in everything."

"He does. And now we've got Le Petite Moreau, if we want it."

Konrad shook his head in disbelief. "It can't be this easy."

Dallas lifted his glass, and Konrad followed suit. "But it is."

"Well, cheers to that."

They clinked glasses and took long, drawn-out sips of the Bloody Marys, which were perfectly spiced.

Konrad placed his glass on the counter. "When can I meet him?" He'd not ever formally met Jacob.

"I told him I'd give him a call on Monday." Dallas took the menu in his hands, reading over it. Konrad already knew what he wanted.

"This is absolutely amazing. I didn't expect to get this news." No. In fact, he'd expected to tell Dallas about his news with Scottie.

"I knew you'd like it." Dallas settled on his stool, the menu back on the bar again. "And the way you walked in here, it looked like you needed some good news."

Dallas was too perceptive for his own good— Konrad's good. Did wanting a woman make a man predictable, make him wear his emotions on his sleeve— or face, as was his case—for everyone to see?

"It happened again. Last night…" Konrad trailed off, his gaze on his friend, who followed him closely without more detail.

"Ty said you didn't show up again last night at H Bar."

"We worked late on a presentation. I had intended to meet the blokes afterward, but that didn't work out."

Dallas took a sip. "I think you're getting caught up with this girl."

Konrad dropped his gaze to his naked wrist. He really missed his watch. "I am."

"Do you want a relationship with her?" Dallas chuckled. "God, I never thought I'd ask *you* that question."

"I never thought I'd have a different answer to that question than 'no fucking way.'" Konrad raked his fingers through his hair. "But now I only know the answer *isn't* no. It's maybe. Bloody hell … no, it's not maybe. It's yes. I do. I do want something with her. But I don't know what or how."

"Fuck, Kon." Dallas didn't say any more until

Bea came back to take their orders.

When she was gone again, Konrad said, "Fucking Fabian and his pussy-whipped ass."

Yes, Konrad still blamed Fabian for falling in love, making it appealing.

"It can't be easy."

Konrad thought about his childhood. "No, it's not. My *Mutter*, the poor girl, didn't fare well. I mean, she would have bent over backward for my father if he'd wanted. And she did. It was always whatever he wanted." He gazed at his manicured fingernails, remembering the times his mother took him with her to have their nails manicured. It was some of the most memorable times of his childhood before his father sent him off to boarding school. "I don't like feeling out of control. This has to be exactly what she felt."

"You worried about it?"

"Fuck yes, I'm worried." Konrad felt anger for his father. For his mother, too. His father had led her to an early grave.

"What's the worst that could happen? You end up like Fabian?"

"No. That Scottie ends up hating me because I don't know how to make a commitment." And worse than that, Konrad would end up hating himself.

"She might hate you already." Dallas laughed, though not in humor. It was his way to lighten the conversation.

"You're probably right." Konrad needed to lighten up. He needed to be rational. He was not his father. He could not hurt anyone out of pure selfishness. "She left my place cross with me last night, but I want to change her mind about me. It that moronic?"

Dallas stared at Konrad, searching his face for several beats before he answered. "I've never seen you like this. So I say no, it's not moronic. You want to be different for her—"

"For myself." He didn't know how to begin. He'd have to wing it.

"Then, definitely, it's not moronic."

Konrad blew out a hefty sigh. He'd hated talking about his feelings. He was lucky Dallas could be a gentleman about it and actually give decent advice, unlike Tylund and Fabian. "I'm going to need about five of these Bloody Marys before brunch is over."

Chapter Twenty

Scottie sat in the kitchen Saturday afternoon, tired because sleep didn't come. It hadn't even been twelve hours since she'd arrived back home, reeling and hating herself. Although she hated the situation more. How could she have let her lust take her by the throat?

Was she just being a fool? An inexperienced idiot who didn't know what to look for in a man? Maybe, because of her prejudices based on her father, she wouldn't know what to do when a good guy came around.

She sighed. Too much was on her mind. She needed to get her life together.

"You're up." Tara walked into the kitchen, holding her iPad.

Scottie glanced up, smiling at her Tara, despite the battle that had been going on inside her. The tension that had been causing them strife had dissipated once Scottie had paid her portion of the rent. Which brought her to another thing she couldn't stop thinking about: her grandmother's brooch—the one she needed to buy back.

"Hey," she replied to Tara's greeting.

"Are you okay?"

Scottie sighed. Not at all. Maybe it was time she stopped pretending she was. "I'm just realizing how hard it is to be an adult."

"Aww, Scott." Tara touched her arm, and Scottie leaned into it.

"I'm sorry about the rent," said Scottie. "I should not have just assumed you'd take care of it. I never expected anything from anyone before. Don't know why I did now."

Tara gazed at her thoughtfully. "Don't say that.

You *can* expect things from people, but you do have to make you own way."

"I know." Scottie looked down at her yogurt and granola bowl. "I appreciate you so much. I hope you know that, Tara."

"I know. And I'm sorry for being such a hard ass about the rent. But I'm on my own. I don't have anyone to rely on. Well, just Brett, though I wouldn't consider him reliable either."

As much as Scottie wanted to express her opinion of Brett, she didn't. It wasn't her place to tell Tara what a complete douche he was. Still, it made her think of Konrad again. Scottie was so confused about where he stood—where she stood. What made it worse was he was her boss. There was no way she'd quit without getting another position first. She'd need another one, stat. But the thing was, she didn't want to quit just yet. She wanted to stay, get to the bottom of it all.

Everything was messed up.

"This is why I don't date," Scottie said, averting her eyes. She still smelled like Konrad. And sex.

"When's the last time you dated someone? Or better yet, had sex?"

Oh God. Konrad's powerful body between her legs giving her life. His soft lips dancing with hers. His velvety tongue against hers. His massive palms holding her thighs apart.

"I don't know…" Scottie was a bit too breathy. She absolutely knew the answer. She still felt the soreness between her legs.

"Has it been since sophomore year? Jonathon?"

Three years, really? The first man she'd had sex with was a nice guy in her intro to biology class. He was safe. And a dud. He should not have been her first. Scottie had always struggled in that area. Men were bad news. She'd seen it growing up with her own father, who had abandoned her, and all the loser boyfriends her mother had had.

"I guess Jon was the last guy I dated." Scottie didn't want to talk about it anymore. She did, however, consider coming clean about Konrad and how much she'd started to fall for him. That was so completely ridiculous, though, that, in the end, she opted to keep it to herself.

Maybe she could act like nothing happened. When she left Korr Properties, either by contract expiration or a new position, she'd surely never seen him again. Never cross paths. Never anything again.

She hated that thought.

"Don't you want a boyfriend?"

She wanted Konrad. In his bed. As her boyfriend.

"No. I'm good. I need to work on myself." The words came out so rehearsed, she almost believed it.

"Oh, come on, Scottie. You've been saying that since collage. Isn't there someone you're interested in?" Tara wasn't going to let it go.

Scottie looked away, standing. She walked to the refrigerator, though didn't open it. "Can't say I am."

"Not even at your new job?" Tara had peeled a banana. "No cuties there?"

Scottie sighed. "Not a one." The conversation was over. Awkwardly, she changed the subject for her own sanity. "Hey, do you need help with any catering gigs? I'm trying to earn some extra cash."

"What do you need extra cash for?" Tara, thankfully, didn't press the boyfriend topic anymore.

Scottie opened the refrigerator, peering at all the leftover boxes and half-drunk bottles of juice and water inside. "I'm trying to get back something I pawned."

"What did you pawn?"

Scottie shrugged, closing the door and facing Tara again, taking in her concern. "Just something I want to get back."

"Did you pawn something to pay rent?" Scottie's refusal to answer made Tara glower. "You didn't."

"It's okay. I can get it back." Scottie waved her hand, although she wasn't totally positive she could get the brooch back.

"Did you pawn what I think you did?" Tara's eyes were intense on hers again.

"Don't worry about it." Scottie walked to the couch, falling into the cushions.

"It was your grandmother's brooch, wasn't it?"

"Yes."

"Damn, Scottie." She walked to the couch, and her hand fell on Scottie's shoulder. "Were you really that desperate?"

The bit of frustration she felt toward Tara stopped at her clenched jaw. "It's okay. I can get it back."

Tara shook her head. "I'm sorry. I had no idea it was that bad. I know how much that brooch means to you."

Tara was the first person Scottie had called when she'd received it. They were silent again. If Scottie said another word, she'd cry.

Nodding, Tara said, "I do need help with another catering job I have tomorrow morning. It's an all-day thing on a yacht."

"A yacht?" Scottie gasped.

"I'm going to get a fat check for the job. If you can help me, I'll give you twenty-five percent."

"No way, Tara!" Scottie's heart raced.

"It's fine. Trust me, I'll have plenty left over. And I think this client likes me. I have another job next Friday through her, so I know there will be more jobs in the future."

Scottie hugged Tara. "Looks like Decadent Chick Catering is finally taking off!"

"I think it is! Finally. Thanks to Antonia and Fabian."

Scottie's heart stalled. "What?"

"You know, the couple we catered on Monday."

"Oh." Scottie brought her fingers to her lips. Konrad would be there.

"Is something wrong?" Tara moved around the couch stood near the edge of the coffee table.

Yes. Very wrong. "No. Not at all."

"So, let's celebrate tonight," Tara said, setting on the couch next to Scottie and taking her hand in hers. "We can't stay out too late though. Have to get up early in the morning."

Scottie could only smile. What was she supposed to do? She needed to stay away from Konrad, especially outside of the office. But would she be able to keep her secret about Konrad under wraps when their private lives kept overlapping?

Chapter Twenty-One

Konrad glanced at his Rolex. Not even eleven, and his eyelids drooped from lack of sleep. The music at H Bar kept him awake though, along with his rowdy friends as they all took a third round of tequila shots. Frankly, Konrad thought Fabian had gone overboard with the engagement celebrations.

Konrad took the shot because he was a sport after all. "That's it, lads. No more tequila for this German."

"You're drinking like a sissy tonight," Tylund said, slamming the shot glass down next to Melina's untouched shot.

"We have had too many shots," Antonia chimed in, accepting a surprise kiss from Fabian.

Get a room. Konrad looked away. If Scottie had been there, she'd be on his lap too, getting surprise kisses at every turn.

"This son of a bitch had half a dozen Bloody Marys at brunch today," Dallas said, laughing.

"Business as usual," Konrad said, glancing at the bar from the VIP nook they'd always reserved. He needed fresh air and water before he imbibed any further. So much for bottle service. "I'll be back."

"Where you going?" Tylund lifted his arms over his head to stretch, pulling on Melina's ponytail in the process. She smacked his thigh.

Why don't those two just shag already?

Clearly, Konrad wasn't in a mood. "To the bar. I need some H_2O." He maneuvered around the low tables, which were solid with liquor bottles and glasses.

Without further hassle from the crew, he made it out of the VIP section and through the main floor. Several people stopped to greet him, mostly acquaintances. Some where women he'd had on rotation at some point or another. Had he only really been in Houston for less than a year? He didn't even want to think how many women he'd bedded since he arrived.

The fresh air finally hit his face when he'd reached an empty spot along the bar. H Bar had been packed as usual on a Saturday night.

The bartender, Victoria, walked over to him right away. She knew him, and he knew her. *Knew* her, knew her.

"Hey, stud. Don't tell me you've emptied all those bottles, have you?" A coquettish smile pulled her bee-stung full lips.

"Not a chance, love. I just needed some air and water. I hope you have some for me." He leaned in, remembering when he'd taken her to the men's room last weekend. Not his best hour.

Victoria bent over to retrieve a bottle of Fiji water from the bar refrigerator. "Glass?"

"Not tonight. I'm going to drink it like an animal." He turned the bottle cap until it snapped open.

"A beast," she said, her blues eyes sparkling.

Before he responded, two arms snaked around his waist from behind. Victoria's eyes dulled at the display. Konrad glanced down at the tanned slim hands around him, wrists ornate with a Cartier industrial bangle he'd purchased. Pilar.

He turned to her, her lips lifted high in a smile. She was alone. "Hi, gorgeous! What are you doing here?"

Pilar squeezed her arms, giving him a real hug. Her face in his chest, she said, "Hey, *guapo*. Just meeting Esteban."

Konrad chuckled. "You better get off me or else he and I will come to blows."

She laughed, looking up to him. She barely came up to his chest. "He's not *loco*."

"I don't know, love. I thought he might have tried something at dinner the other night."

She shook her head, her smile warm and comfortable. He'd truly grown fond of her. "You look good. Are you feeling better?"

He wrapped his arms around her, strengthening their friendly embrace. "I'm okay." He leaned down to kiss her forehead, his lips lingering there, but his gaze drifted. Right to a pair of hazel eyes planted on him from across the bar.

Scottie.

Fuck. Me. Konrad didn't expect to see her until the Sunday brunch. He'd still not sorted out what he'd say to her. How he'd tell her she was wrong about him.

He released his arms fast. Scottie was faster and spun on her heels to go in the opposite direction to the ladies' room. As she did so, the catering chef Tara came into view, a lanky guy holding on to her waist. But it wasn't only them. Jeff came into view, too, watching Scottie. Calling to her.

A kick in the balls would hurt less. Why the hell was Jeff with her? If they were on a date, Konrad would die. The notion made him absolutely ill.

He left the bar. Left his water behind. Left Pilar calling to him. His only mission was to get to Scottie.

In his mad race to her, he passed Jeff, not acknowledging him, though he himself had been acknowledged. Down the dark hall to the bathroom, he spotted Scottie holding the ladies' room door knob. She froze at the sight of him. Her eyes first widened in surprise, then narrowed to slits.

He came on her like a lunatic, taking her face in in his palms as if he had the right to do it. "What are you doing?"

She shoved his hands away. "What are *you* doing?" Her voice cracked.

"Here with Jeff, are you?" He glanced back. Still alone. His heartbeat reverberated in his ears. His whole body thumped from his hard pulse. "It didn't take you long, did it?"

Her forehead creased, a blaze in her eyes making her irises glow green in the dim light. "Seriously? *You* obviously are here with Pilar. So it didn't take *you* long, did it?"

He reached for her again, his hands on her face again, pulling her into a kiss she succumbed to for a microsecond before she pushed away from him again.

"Don't kiss me with those lips." She brought a trembling hand to her mouth, wiping it.

He'd never been in such a high emotional situation. Control was gone. Nothing was his deliberate doing. Everything sprang forth from the turmoil flowing inside, the ache, the loss of stability. He had no idea who he was in that moment, but he knew he didn't want Scottie to walk away from him. And he didn't want her to be with anyone else. Nothing was clearer than that, even when everything else was very unclear.

"Are you with him, Scottine?" His voice croaked.

"No, you asshole! I'm not with him." She shook her head. "We ran into him at Bowie Brew and he followed us here."

The way she looked at him made him want to fall through the floor and never return. If Scottie thought he was scum, then everyone did. "I'm not with Pilar. I'm with my friends."

"Oh, right." She glanced past him at the sounds of heels tapping on the tiles.

Konrad took her hand and pulled her a few feet to

the corner of the hall, where the wall met another wall. She yanked her hand away. He took it back, bringing it to his lips. "I swear, I'm not with Pilar. I ended it with her before we got together."

She didn't pull her hand away. "I don't believe you, Konrad."

"Look at me, Scottie." He pressed her back against the wall, his body sizzling for her, wanting her so bad, wanting to taste her lips again—be inside her again. When she didn't look, he demanded it again.

Hazel eyes met his. "What?" The simple question was all breath.

"I…" He stared at her, taking in every part of her face: her eyes, her nose, her quivering lips, her exposed décolleté, the pulse at her throat. "I think it's you."

"What's me?" Her voice cracked.

"What I want. I want you."

She gasped at his words.

"Do you want me too?"

Her lips parted. She looked as stunned as he was by his words, but she didn't respond, didn't give him the "yes" he wanted to hear. She didn't say no, either.

Konrad pressed his lips against hers in a hard kiss. As harsh as he was with her, she wrapped her arms around him. Their kiss grew in strength, in undeniable power—in an intensity he'd never known before.

She pulled away before he could completely lose his mind with her. "I have to get back. They'll come looking for me."

As much as he didn't want to, he released her but caged her in with his hand on the wall. "I have half a mind to not care." But he had to. Jeff was his employee, and Konrad and Scottie needed to talk about what this all meant.

She glanced past him. "You have to care."

Leaning in to kiss her again before he set her free, he said, "I know."

Their kiss lasted longer than it should have. When they parted, a voice called from the end of the hall.

"Look who it is!" Jeff walked up, thankfully seeming to have missed the display of only seconds ago.

Scottie stepped away from Konrad, smoothing back her wild hair. "We just ran into each other."

Jeff had a smirk on his lips. Perhaps he'd seen something after all. "Yeah, I saw him walk by. What a surprise, Lord Korr."

"Fancy meeting you here. I was just saying that to Scottie, wasn't I?"

Nodding, she said, "He was."

Jeff's gaze slid from Konrad to Scottie. "We were wondering where you ran off to, Scottie. Tara thought you saw someone you knew."

"Oh, yeah. No. Actually, I just had a wardrobe emergency." She laughed nervously. "All better now."

"We got a table," said Jeff. "Come join us." He didn't look back to Konrad, who wanted to obliterate Jeff when he reached for her arm.

Scottie moved, avoiding his hold. "Let's go then." She looked back at Konrad, her eyes telling him so much. She did want him. He didn't need her verbal yes.

Konrad walked behind them, and as they remerged into the noisy main bar, he leaned in to her as he passed and said into her ear, "Your lips are mine."

He continued to walk to the VIP section and didn't look back.

Chapter Twenty-Two

Your lips are mine. Konrad's words kept Scottie up all night. Six in the morning came fast, and as lethargic as her body was, her mind soared. She'd never known excitement like this for a man before. She'd never felt the sick, but good sick, feeling in her stomach, never been consumed with fantasies about a man. Konrad was the first.

All her fears were pushed aside. She didn't care how fast it seemed. These things happened fast sometimes. At least that was what she'd heard before. Her mother once moved a man into their apartment after knowing him just two weeks. Finally, Scottie understood what drove a person to do such things.

She got up from her bed, eyes scanning her all-black outfit for the catering job. With two hundred dollars left over from pawning the brooch, she needed a thousand to get the pin back. This propelled her forward. She felt light on her feet and in her spirit as she flounced around her room, getting her things together. A notification on her cell phone stopped her in her tracks. The text could only be from one person.

Konrad: *Schatzi*, **will I see you today on the yacht?**

Me: **Yes.**

Scottie's body surged. She couldn't wait to see him again.

Konrad: **Good. I'll kidnap you for a little while. Maybe no one will notice. Is that okay with you?**

Scottie bit her lip. Was this really happening? Was she really doing this? With Konrad? The man she wanted to stay away from? The man she had helped break hearts?

Yes.

Me: **I want that**.

Another text chimed her phone.

Konrad: **Good. I hope you're ready for me.**

She tingled deep within, thinking of all the ways she'd be ready for him.

Tara called Scottie, taking her attention. She walked into the kitchen, taking an apron to the face again. Groaning, Scottie tied it around her waist, and thought of the texts messages with Konrad she'd just had.

"What's with you?" Tara tilted her head. "You're actually smiling. It's weird."

I should tell her. What was the harm in telling Tara that Konrad was her boss? It seemed crazy not to.

"Umm…" Scottie picked at the screen print of Decadent Chick Catering on the apron. "Okay, so… So, this might be weird…"

"Not weirder than you're being right now, Scott. What's going on?"

Dropping her hands to her sides, she began, "So, you know my boss at the temp job?"

"Yeah…"

"It's one of Fabian's friends. Konrad Korr. The tall blond." It sounded like no big deal in Scottie's head. She hoped that was how Tara took it.

Not likely.

"You're shitting me." Tara shook her head in disbelief, her hands coming up to her face. "And you didn't say anything? *Y'all* didn't say anything? Why?"

"I really didn't think you'd cater for them again. Sorry." Scottie knew Tara would not be satisfied with her answer.

"Seriously?" Tara gripped the edge of the counter. "Scottie, if this *is* a weird thing—"

"It's not!"

Tara studied Scottie's face. "Fine." She bent over, closing the cooler lids. "God, just when things were smooth sailing. You better tell me immediately if it gets awkward."

"It won't." Scottie was feeling more confident that day than she had in a while.

When they arrived at the marina in Kemah, Texas, Scottie spotted Fabian waiting for them on the edge of the dock. With him was a captain and another crew member dressed in a uniform of white shorts and a navy polo shirt.

Fabian smiled at them as they approached carrying the lighter boxes. "Good morning, ladies! Do you have more in the car?"

"Yes. A lot more," Tara said, handing him a box.

"Greggory will get the rest of it. Is that your SUV?" He pointed to the SUV parked next to a Bentley, which was clearly his. Greggory, the crew member, took both boxes and disappeared down the ramp, Tara at his side.

"Come. Let me show you around." Fabian briefly touched Scottie's elbow. "You're Scottie, right?"

"Yes, Scottie Roberts."

"I'm Fabian Pallis. My better half, Antonia, should be here any minute."

"Your fiancée is very beautiful. She'll make a stunning bride." Scottie felt weird talking to Fabian.

Fabian nodded. "She is amazing."

She glanced at him, taking in his expression. Everything that was hard and angled about his face softened. This big, muscular, strong man had turned to complete mush at the mention of his fiancée. Scottie knew that was the look of love. It was beautiful and made her feel hopeful for once in her life.

When they'd finally reached a full-sized kitchen in the labyrinth that was the yacht, he turned to face her. "This is the main kitchen. Set up here."

He pointed to the long counter space and the island in the middle. It was larger than the kitchen she and Tara shared. The display of wealth was outright obscene.

"Okay. Where will you and your guests have brunch?" She lifted the box that had been put on the floor.

"The upper deck has a table set up for ten. We'll have brunch there. The buffet will be there too, but I would like for you to come around and refill drinks as needed."

"Of course. We are here for your every need." She pulled her hair up, her heart fluttering.

He winked, his white smile emerging from his tan face. "That's what I like to hear."

"So, I'll let you get to it." Fabian pulled the sunglasses from his polo pocket and slipped them on before he left her in the kitchen.

Thirty minutes later, Scottie balanced a tray of mimosas on one hand and a tray of mini almond raisin cinnamon rolls on the other.

"Just don't drop them," Tara called over her shoulder, busy chopping and seasoning and performing her culinary magic.

"I won't." She took one step at a time until out of the kitchen and into a living room decorated in a nautical theme of stripes, shiny Cherrywood, and chrome finishes.

"Watch your step, love." The voice came from the left.

Before she could rebalance or catch a breath, both trays went crashing down to the floor, drenching her—

and the ottoman nearby—with sticky orange mimosa.

"Shit!" she screamed.

His lip curled up in humor. "Indeed."

Scottie met Konrad's eyes, and she knew exactly what he was thinking because she was thinking the same thing. He reached for her, his mouth crashing down on hers with a passion that made her feel weightless.

With lips against hers, he said, "God, you look adorable in an apron. I want you to wear this later and nothing else."

"Stop," she whispered, pressing into his kiss again.

When they parted, he looked down at her. "Am I dreaming?"

She took in every part of his face. "No."

He moaned, his nose dipping down to her neck. "Good."

Tara's voice stopped them from falling into each other further. Good thing. Scottie needed to remember what she was doing. And who she was doing it with. They separated quickly.

"Scottie?" Tara walked in, her eyes narrowed. "Oh…" She surveyed the mess of orange mimosa and mini cinnamon rolls all over an extremely expensive-looking ottoman. "What the hell happened?"

Konrad dropped to his knees, picking up the champagne flutes and rolls on the floor. "It's my fault. I smashed into her."

Scottie kneeled next to him, helping him clean up. "No, it was me. I should have watched what I was doing."

To make matters worse, Fabian and Antonia walked in then, getting an eyeful of the scene. Fabian gasped. "What happened here?"

"No worries, mate. I ran into Scottie," Konrad

repeated, glancing at Scottie.

Fabian's eyebrows lifted.

"I did it. It was me." Scottie would take the responsibility.

"Rubbish. She's being nice."

"Stop cleaning, Konrad. What's the matter with you?" Fabian said, annoyed.

"I'll get the maid." Antonia left, calling out to someone named Emily.

Konrad stood. "Come on, Scottie." Offering her his hand, she took it, letting him pull her to her feet.

"I'm so sorry about this." Tara was mortified. "We'll replace the ottoman."

"Don't worry about it. I'll square it with Fabian."

Scottie couldn't believe how determined he was to protect her, and it made her chest swell with warmth. The more she looked at him, the more she really *saw* him, the more she knew she was in trouble. Her heart could not deny it. Everything she'd believed about Konrad and men had been turned on its head with that look.

Before Fabian climbed back up the stairs, he asked Konrad to join him on the upper deck. Konrad nodded, though he stayed behind. Scottie wondered if he would tell Tara their secret. The big secret.

"Wow," Tara began, wiping her hands on the apron tied around her waist. "This *is* awkward." She threw Scottie a disapproving glance.

"I told her you're my boss." Scottie decided to take control of the situation. In doing so, she took a step back from Konrad. They looked too close, too intimate. She wasn't ready to tell Tara the other secret.

"I don't see why you have to keep that a secret." Tara was annoyed.

"It's not a secret. Yes, Scottie works for me.

There's no problem."

Thank God.

"Exactly." Scottie had unprecedented mixed feelings about his rationale. Though she knew he couldn't disclose everything, in some irresponsible way, she wanted him to claim her.

"No worries, Tara. This doesn't affect anything," Konrad said smoothly.

Tara seemed satisfied. "I'm glad to hear it." Tara bent over the ottoman, picking up the last of the mess. "Scottie, help me clean this up."

"Leave it. Emily will be here any moment." Konrad stuck his hand out in front of Scottie.

Tara sighed, standing. "Okay. Thank you, Konrad. Hopefully I haven't completely ruined any chance for future catering jobs."

"Trust me, you haven't. In fact, I'll bet you've earned more." He smiled.

Scottie followed Tara back into the gourmet kitchen, Konrad still in her mind.

Chapter Twenty-Three

"So, she works for you at Korr Properties?" Fabian lifted his eyebrows.

Konrad glanced at Scottie holding a tray of salmon puffs to Antonia and two of her friends across the upper deck where they'd been tanning for hours. They'd been cruising toward the Gulf of Mexico at full speed, the water lapping against the sides of the yacht.

"Yes." *Damn, she's gorgeous*. Konrad couldn't take his eyes off Scottie. She was the only woman he could see.

"And you knew," Fabian continued, his finger pointed at Dallas accusingly.

Dallas lifted his hands in surrender. "Hey, it wasn't my business to tell."

"She's hot," Tylund put in, his gaze on her too. Konrad wanted to shove him overboard.

"Don't," Konrad sniped, causing eyebrows to lift further.

Not Dallas though. He had a sagacious look in his eyes.

Konrad shoved his sunglasses to the top of his head. "I'd rather you not objectify my employee," he said to Tylund.

"Or he'll be forced to defend her." Dallas grinned.

Konrad pushed down his sunglasses over his eyes again. The Coast Guard would be busy fetching Konrad's friends out of the Gulf if they kept it up.

Wankers. Konrad turned his gaze back to Scottie. She was more than hot. His eyes followed her lines, curving and petite. He relived his touch on her skin, making him hard almost instantly. He wanted her again.

169

And she must have sensed him staring because her eyes shifted to him, her wide smile taming into a coy curve on her lips. They were on the same wavelength. No question.

"Excuse me, lads. I'm going to fetch a salmon puff before the ladies devour them all." Without waiting for a response, he made his way to her.

"Konrad!" Melina called upon his arrival, her champagne flute lifted. She'd already had a whole bottle herself. "Cheers!"

"Cheers, love!" His eyes were on Scottie.

"Salmon puff?" Scottie lifted the tray.

"I'd love one." He took a puff and brought it to his lips, reveling in her attention to his every move.

Scottie seemed embarrassed to be caught staring because her cheeks blushed, and she looked away. "I better get more." She dashed off, leaving him to quickly devise a plan to get her alone.

Because Konrad knew the layout of Fabian's yacht well, he retreated back inside from the opposite end, knowing it would lead to the same wide staircase back to the main cabin. He waited for Scottie at the bottom, scanning the area. He was completely alone.

Seconds later, her shoes tapped against each step until she became aware of him. Stopping in her tracks, she gasped.

"Konrad." His name was breathy on her lips.

Without a word, he took her face in his hands and kissed her so hard, she dropped the tray. The crashing sound parted them, but his attention wasn't on the tray. Neither was hers.

"I'm kidnapping you." He was breathing heavily, his groin tightening in response to her finger hooked in his belt loop.

"Now?" She glanced toward the kitchen. "We

can't here. Can we?"

"Not here." He took her hand. "Come with me."
Without resisting, she squeezed her fingers around his
and let him lead.

In the wing of bedroom cabins, Konrad opened a
door to one he'd stayed in many times. The urgency to be
together was so strong, he didn't glance inside. He didn't
take notice of the furniture or any other detail inside the
room. All his focus was on her hand riding up his
forearm.

He closed the door, pushing her back against it.
"My God, Scottie. This is absolute torture." He pressed
his mouth on hers, taking her tongue between his lips.

She put her hand on his chest, separating their
connection. "Will they hear us?"

"Not a chance." Konrad picked her up in one fell
swoop, his lips still on hers, and walked to the king bed
in the center of the large cabin. He placed her on the bed,
trying to contain himself. Desire took over.

Once on the bed, Scottie pawed his polo shirt,
lifting it over his ribcage, and tossed it to ground when
she'd succeeded.

"I was serious about the apron." After he'd untied
her apron, he yanked it off, and she slipped under him,
taking his bottom lip between her teeth. He loved how
responsive she was to him. It matched exactly what he
felt for her. Ready. Urgent. And he was so fucking hard.
He would rip the crotch of his shorts if he didn't get them
off.

Through their fast, hungry need for each other,
they'd stripped off each other's clothes until they were
naked. He ran his palm down the center of her chest until
he touched her clit. Scottie spread her legs wider,
hooking her legs around him. He hovered over her,
staring into her sun-touched face, his heart slowing way

down. He knew they had to be fast, but that didn't stop his desire to savor her.

Konrad kissed her neck, sucking her skin while he rubbed her. Her whimpers kept him going, kept him on the path to her pleasure. He took her nipple in his mouth, licking it, biting it, and only pulling back when she winced.

"Sorry," he said on a groan, his mouth moving toward her other nipple. "I can't help it."

"No. It's okay. You didn't hurt me." Her pelvis lifted to his circling touch.

Another bite to her nipple and she bucked under him.

"You taste good," he said. The task to get down her body continued. Down her stomach, he circled his tongue on her sweet skin, dipping it into her belly button. He intended to go farther.

"Oh…" She moaned as he slipped a finger inside her.

Wet and hot, the thought of being inside her made him absolutely insane. He already knew what it felt like, but there was something that felt different about being there with her on the yacht. The anticipation of having her, of making her orgasm so hard the whole yacht might find out about them, got him more excited, if that were possible. That was his lust talking, though.

He didn't want to think about the others on the yacht. There were no others, as far as he was concerned. How different his life could be in a week astounded him.

He moved down still, his mouth between her thighs. She was bare and completely open to him. Glancing up, he met her eyes, which were drooping with wanton need. She'd never looked so gorgeous. Taking his lower lip between his teeth, he turned his gaze back to her.

"I'm going to taste you," he said, his palms pushing down her thighs. A moan soared through the air, and he nearly lost it.

One swipe, then two, and her skin sent him ablaze. He couldn't stop himself. He intended to lick every part of her. Over and over, he circled his tongue around her. He delved his tongue inside her, making her buck under him, soft words falling from her lips he didn't quite decipher over the hard beat of the blood coursing between his ears.

"Konrad..." she cried, her fingers fisting his hair. She was close. He could feel it. "Please. Please..."

He continued licking her and rubbing her. She was his priority. It has always been that way with her. No one else had ever been able to evoke that from him.

Scottie stilled. Didn't move a muscle. Didn't make a sound. Didn't breathe. Faster, his tongue moved over her, feeling the hard intensity of her impending orgasm.

"Come on, Scottine," he murmured, his mouth back to the task.

One more flick, and she let herself go. Releasing his hair, she grabbed a pillow and pulled it over her face. Her attempt at discretion didn't stop his tongue. He continued until she pushed his head away.

"No more," she panted, staring down at him from under the pillow.

"Oh, there will be more. I promise you that."

Tossing the pillow from her face, he kissed her with a savage appetite that wasn't nearly quelled. Tasting her had made his erection harder than it was before. He sprung off the bed, finding his shorts on the floor. Rummaging through his wallet, he pulled out a condom. He'd come prepared.

Scottie was on her haunches, passion darkening

her eyes. She reached for the packet. "Let me."

She sheathed him quickly and was on her back again. Between her legs, Konrad entered her rough and fast. He groaned with the resistance around him. Hot waves moved through him, making him feel alive. Closing his eyes, he buried himself deep inside her until their stomachs touched. Scottie cried out, biting his shoulder.

"You feel tremendous," he said, choking on his words. He'd never felt so uninhibited or free.

He moved inside her, slow at first, then faster. She wrapped her legs around him, pulling him as close to her as he could. There was such comfort there against her skin. And ease. He wasn't thinking of work or getting back to his mates. Those were the last things on his mind.

Her breath hitched, and he knew she was getting close again. A smile pulled at his lips. Yes, he could pleasure her like this all day. Of that, he was positive. Sensing her need for him to quicken his pace, he did.

"Oh, God, Konrad," she said through rapid breaths and groans. "I'm close again."

"Good," he growled against her forehead, kissing her smooth skin.

Not even a second later, she came undone, and he reveled in her sounds. In her body wrapping itself around him. In the thought that he could take her to pleasure so easily and intended to do it every chance he got.

It wasn't long until his pending orgasm ripped through him, and he was tensing his muscles, pacing himself until a mass of explosions whipped through him. "Fuck…"

A sense of calm took him. He'd never been so satisfied.

He gathered she hadn't either by the way she lay there, holding him in her steady arms, and by the way she pressed little kisses against his shoulder.

Bending, he kissed her with appreciation. It was passionate. It was the most intense kiss he'd ever shared with someone.

During the kiss, he knew he wanted to get used to it. He wanted to memorize how she moved against him. How she tasted. How she danced in rhythm with him. And more than that, he didn't want to mess up with her.

They parted, and she said, "I think I've been gone too long."

As much as he hated to let her go, he knew she was right. "I need you for hours."

"Hours?" She grinned with the prospect.

"A whole weekend, actually." He dipped his head and kissed her again. He rubbed the length of her thigh. "I want you to stay with me tonight."

"What about work on Monday?"

"We'll drive in together." As soon as he said it, he knew he was being too careless. He didn't want his employees to get the wrong idea if they saw them driving in together. What would that do for Scottie's reputation? No, he couldn't risk it. Not while she was still his temp. "Or you can drive from my house if you want. But you're staying over."

She was pensive, looking past him. "Okay. I want to."

"Good." For the first time, he believed he could actually do the relationship thing. And though it scared the shit out of him, he didn't want to run away.

Chapter Twenty-Four

Midnight came. Curled up in Konrad's arms, Scottie didn't expect to feel so comfortable. They were completely different people than they were a week ago.

He stroked her shoulder, eliciting a steady stream of sensations running along her spine.

"Why are you catering?" A smile curled his lips. "You are quite bad at it."

She smacked his arm. "I am not!"

He leaned down to kiss her.

When it was over, she was in such a pure place of emotions, she couldn't lie. "I know. I'm the worst."

He brushed his fingers through her tangled hair. "So, why are you then?"

Scottie grew silent, though the urge to tell him bubbled inside her. If anyone had purchased her grandmother's brooch before she could, she'd be devastated. "Just to help out Tara."

A pause drew out between her words and his. "You're not a good liar, *Schatzi*."

Not at all. And especially not then. She didn't respond.

"Scottie?"

Obviously, he was concerned, and she hated holding it in. If she told him about her grandmother's pin, she'd have to admit that she was not like any women he'd ever been with. And she wondered why she cared so much about their very different financial situations.

She met his gaze. "I sold something to Space City Pawn, and I'm just trying to get it back." Simple enough, though the feelings that tore through her were complicated.

He narrowed his gaze. "Is the agency not paying

you enough of the hourly rate we are paying them?"

Her rate was average for a person just out of college with her experience, which was basically none. However, the question caught her off guard. She didn't know how to respond.

"You should work for Korr Properties permanently." It was a demand, albeit a light demand.

She sat up, holding the sheet close to her chest. "You can't hire me." She felt frantic and totally neurotic about her reaction.

He sat up as well. "Why not?"

It all was so easy to him. He could make a decision, and then it would happen. She didn't have that luxury. "Because the agency won't let me work for you permanently without a huge fee."

His eyebrows lifted. "And...?"

No, she couldn't work for Konrad permanently. That wouldn't solve her problems. It might make them worse, considering she didn't know what being in his bed meant to him. Or her.

"No." She shook her head. "No. That's not a good idea."

Silence fell between them again. Could he really think it was an option? After everything that had happened? After everything yet to happen?

Scottie lay back on the bed. Konrad followed suit. The conversation wasn't over though.

"What did you sell?"

She closed her eyes. *I don't want to talk about this.* "My grandmother's brooch."

"The one you wore with the red dress?"

She smiled, but it faded. "Yes."

Konrad wrapped his arms around her, pulling her into him. It all felt like a dream. "Are you having money problems?"

He asked it as if he already knew the answer. The heat of embarrassment made her kick her leg from under the sheets.

"It's more of a shortage, but I'm fine now." Lie. The truth was harder to say.

"If you're fine, why are you catering? I know it's not really just to help Tara."

"As soon as I make enough, I'll buy back the brooch and quit moonlighting. Or *day*lighting." An awkward, forced laugh came out of her. Who the hell was she? What was she trying to prove?

His lips grazed her shoulder, stirring her desire for him again. Scottie wanted to focus on their desire and not how much she struggled financially.

Against her skin, he said, "Let me buy back the brooch for you."

Every muscle froze, except her heart. It beat three-fold. This seemed too familiar. Quickly, she turned to face him with a rising anger that she didn't know was there waiting under the surface. "No."

"Why?" He seemed amused at her reaction, and it pissed her off.

"Because this is my problem. I need to take responsibility." Honesty felt great. But there was more she needed to say.

His eyes were intense on her, but she wasn't going to back down from his request. "How much?"

"Stop, Konrad. I'm not Anisette or Tamsin. Or Pil—"

"No, *you* stop, Scottie." He furrowed his brow, his own anger coming forth—as it should. She'd dealt an unfair blow that he didn't deserve.

Panic seized her at the look in his eyes. He might walk away. "Why would you want to buy it back for me anyway?"

Konrad sat up, swinging his legs off the bed. Not looking back at her, he said, "Because I can."

Of course. He could do anything he wanted. Have anything he wanted.

"Well, I can't allow it," she said. She sat up too, her emotions roiling about. "I mean, what are we to each other anyway?" And there it was, the real question that spurred all the frustration inside her. Why did she need something definitive from him? Why couldn't she just do as she'd said and enjoy what unfolded with him?

He sighed, his head falling back for a moment. "The fact that you're here in my bed should say what we are."

But she didn't know what that meant. How many women did he have in his bed before her? She was inconveniently reminded of who he was: a player. But things were different now, and she might be pushing him too far. This situation was new to her. She didn't know how to be with someone, didn't know how to make someone want to stay.

"I've never had any other woman in my bed before. But I want *you* in my bed. I like you, Scottie. I want to see where this goes."

Her heart slowed, his words rolling in her mind. Truth was, she believed him. She didn't feel like just another on his list. And she was completely screwing it up.

"I'm sorry." She crawled across the big bed, embracing him from behind. "I feel like I'm in a whirlwind."

"Me too, *Schatzi*."

She kissed his shoulders, the back of his neck, and ran her palms down his biceps.

"I'm bad at this." Her heart throbbed. God, she was so bad, so inexperienced. Her dad should have stuck around, taught her how to relate to men. Clearly, her mother had been a terrible teacher and example.

"You're not the only one." His voice was low. And sad.

He maneuvered her until he was on his back and she straddled him. With his guidance, he was inside her again and she rode him slowly unto the early hours of Monday morning.

****

At seven in the morning, Scottie woke to Konrad singing in the shower. In *German*. With a laugh on her kiss-swollen lips, she tossed back sheets and slipped off the bed that had been their haven. And though she'd had little to no sleep, she felt more refreshed than she ever had.

She padded across the still-dark master bedroom and into the attached bathroom. The size of the room captivated her again, though she'd been in it several times throughout the night. Her whole duplex could fit inside Konrad's master suite. Bare feet to moist tiles, she waded through the stream-filled room.

Konrad's voice grew louder and sharper with each German word, and she couldn't help but giggle at his voracity for the lyrics he belted out.

The singing stopped. "Scottine?"

Still giggling, she could hardly get the question out. God, she'd never felt so happy. "How did you know?"

"I know everything, *Schatzi*," he said with a laugh.

She opened the fogged glass door of the shower stall, complete with a built-in stone bench and eight shower heads. Her gaze moved to a screen mounted on the wall, water droplets gliding down it. Not many, though. It displayed the penthouse floor plan. "I see that!"

"Sharp, right?" He waggled his eyebrows. "No one's catching me with my trousers down!"

She laughed again. "I guess not."

His beautifully naked body gleamed with water caressing his skin. Shampoo suds fluttered off his hair like snow. "Join me, yes?"

The apex of her thighs throbbed in remembrance of all the positions he'd had her in. And hell yes, she wanted to be in more of them in that very obscene and spacious shower. "God, I want to."

His eyes lit up. "Come on, then."

Scottie bit her lip, looking at his thick, muscular body waiting for her to touch. "I have to go back home to get ready for the office."

He frowned, hands back in his hair to corral the shampoo that had drifted down his forehead. "I told you to bring an overnight bag. Didn't I?"

"I know." Her gaze fell over his erection that had softened a bit but was still impressive. She swallowed heavily. At first, she wasn't sure what to expect. There was still a part of her that questioned all of this being real. She'd been waiting for the other shoe to drop. "Next time."

"Tonight." It was a command. One that she'd obey.

"Yes, Lord Korr." She giggled.

He went to her, his wet, soapy body soaking her as his lips came down on hers, his tongue slipping in her willing mouth.

"I'll see you at the office." It took every bit of her energy to separate from him.

****

Back at her duplex, Tara sat in the living room sipping from a coffee cup. She thumbed through a planner, randomly jotting notes every few seconds.

Scottie's stomach rippled with anxiety. She'd never spent a night away from home. Tara would question her, and Scottie didn't know what to say. Slowly, as if she might have a chance to go unnoticed, Scottie put one foot into the tiny hall leading to the bedrooms.

"You were at Konrad's, weren't you?"

Scottie stopped, knowing she'd never really had a chance in hell of succeeding.

Time to face the music. She had to come clean about everything. It was the only way, but she still wasn't sure if she could. If she did, then it really would be real, and she would be doing the thing she swore she wouldn't do: want to be with a playboy.

Scottie slung her purse on the back of the couch. "What do you mean?"

Tara's eyebrows lifted. She didn't seem impressed. In fact, she looked downright pissed. Offended too. "Scottie, don't bullshit me."

Scottie wished she would have taken an overnight bag, wished her damn insecurity hadn't gotten the best of her. "I wouldn't bullshit you." What was so wrong in her decision to be with a man? Was she afraid, in being with Konrad, she'd be just like her mom? *Oh God.* Maybe... But, she knew it wasn't true. She was not her mom. And Konrad was not her father.

Tara closed her datebook. With eyes steady and infiltrating, she stared at Scottie, probably reading her thoughts, as she did so many times. "Please don't lie to me."

"I'm not lying." *Just say the words.* Scottie looked away. Konrad was right. She was a horrible liar.

"I saw you two on the yacht. You came out of one of the cabins together." Tara forced Scottie to look at her, and shook her head disapprovingly. "You and your *boss.* Tell me I'm wrong."

Scottie's silence said it all.

"God, Scottie." Tara let out an exasperated sigh. "What are you doing?"

Anger filled Scottie, but she repressed it. "We like each other."

Tara snorted. "He's your boss."

Scottie hated when she got all self-righteous. "Yeah, I know that, Tara. Thanks for reminding me." She wanted to get out from under Tara's judgmental eyes. Why couldn't Tara support her? Encourage her?

Tara's face softened, her pursed lips replaced by a slight curve. "Scottie, you can't be involved with him."

Scottie crossed her arms over her chest. Finally, after all the nagging she'd received about staying away from men, she'd found the nagging continued because it wasn't the right man in Tara's eyes. This was Scottie's decision. She refused to feel bad about it, despite what Tara or anyone else would think. "And why not?"

"You work for him."

"Is this really about you? About you worried I might have screwed up any chances you have to get jobs with Konrad's friends?" Scottie had had it with Tara's judgment.

Tara shook her head, more determined than ever. "I looked him up online."

"So?" Scottie dropped her hands. The conversation was over as far as she was concerned.

"He has a lot of women. A lot." Tara added quickly, "You won't be the only one, and I'm afraid you're going to be hurt. Really hurt."

"Maybe I'm not afraid." Scottie's hands were shaking. "Maybe I want to see where it goes with him."

"It's not going to go anywhere." Tara wasn't

backing down. Or stopping. "Do you want to see the pictures I found? He's bedded half of River Oaks, and he hasn't even been in Houston for a year yet!"

Scottie lifted her hand. "Stop."

"Scott—"

"Why don't you worry about *your* relationship and let me figure out mine." Scottie turned, dueling emotions of anger and grief bringing tears to her eyes. Tara didn't know Konrad. No one did. Scottie saw a glimpse of the real him, and she wasn't going to give it up.

Chapter Twenty-Five

Konrad walked into the office at eight in the morning with a spring in his step. Everything he felt that morning, he'd attributed it to Scottie. The idea of having her in his bed again that night excited him more than he could have anticipated. It felt great. He was on top of the world. What had he really been afraid of all these years? His parents' mistakes weren't his, and he wouldn't allow them to form his future anymore.

"Good morning, Konrad." The voice came from behind him just as he passed the reception desk.

Konrad turned. Marisol, his regular assistant who was on maternity leave, stood there with a stroller, the one he'd bought for her. She beamed at him so brightly, he couldn't contain his own smile. "Marisol, love!"

"Hi there."

He put his briefcase on the reception desk. Susan, who had been on the phone, pulled it over the desk. Konrad strode to Marisol, his gaze fixed on the stroller. "You've brought some precious cargo, I see."

"Thanks to you, Kon." She accepted his hug. "I'm sorry it's taken me so long to thank you for your gifts. It's been tough this last week."

He peered at the sleeping baby, and his heart warmed. He was once that peaceful. "No worries, Mari."

"I thought I would come by and introduce everyone to my little Andres."

"Andres," Konrad repeated. "That's a fine name for a tyke."

Marisol laughed quietly. "He's something special."

"Looks like it."

Susan walked over. "Isn't he lovely, Konrad?"

"Absolutely." He continued to stare down at the child, emotions roiling inside him. He hoped the child had all the love he needed and more. There was nothing worse than neglect. He knew that too well.

"It's true what they say," Marisol began, her gaze on her baby. "I never would have understood it before, but I am not the same person since this one came into my life. I can never be the same."

"You're a mommy," Susan said.

Konrad's heart throbbed, and he wondered if he'd be different too. And then he wondered why he'd thought about being a father. He'd never thought it before. He changed the subject. "So, are you back to work then?"

The women laughed.

"He's got a nice, young temp," Susan directed to Marisol. "She has him wrapped around her finger."

Konrad met Marisol's all-knowing gaze. "She's exaggerating. You know you're the only one for me, Mari."

"I don't know…" Susan shrugged. "He took her to the EaDo Property and gave her a tour of Korr Solutions *himself.* When has he ever given any one of us a tour of Korr Solutions?"

"Wait a minute. You took her to the EaDo Property? I haven't even seen it!" Marisol lifted an eyebrow.

"I thought she needed some context." Konrad needed to be more careful.

"Speak of the darling," Susan said, making Konrad's gaze travel to the door where Scottie had walked through.

Scottie wore a fitted white dress that grazed her knees. Her dark hair was pulled back in a ponytail, emphasizing her bright eyes, more green than brown in the fluorescent light.

"Darling, indeed," Marisol said under her breath.

"Shut up, the both of you," Konrad muttered. He'd hoped his heart was not in his eyes as he watched her. Scottie completely took his breath away.

She paused before them. "Good morning."

"Scottie, this is Marisol." Konrad pointed to the stroller. "And this is her baby, Andres."

"Nice to meet you. I promise I'm not messing up your desk." She laughed, peering into the stroller.

Marisol caught Konrad's eyes for a second before turning her attention to Scottie. "It's all good. Mess away."

"Cute baby." Scottie grinned down at his little chubby face as he stirred.

"Thank you."

"Well, walk around. Show off that fine boy of yours. I've got to get to it." Konrad walked toward the desk to retrieve his briefcase.

"I'll drop by your office before I leave," Marisol called to him.

"Sounds good. Scottie, I need you in my office." Konrad didn't look back at the women. He could only guess what they were thinking. Yes, Scottie had him very much wrapped around her finger.

"Of course," Scottie said, walking closely behind him.

In his office, he put his briefcase on his desk. "Close the door." He listened until the door clicked shut. Without looking at her, he said, "How am I supposed to work when your ass looks quite tasty in that white dress?"

"Umm…" Luscious lips curled up, making him instantly hard.

"I'm going to ruin that dress. I hope you realize that."

"Konrad…" She was breathless.

He looked up, meeting her languid gaze. "Are you wearing panties?"

She bit her lip. He grew harder still, like a schoolboy. Scottie made him feel young again, like he could start over.

Just as she was about to respond, the intercom buzzed. "Konrad?"

Scottie pressed her lips together. He held up his hand when she attempted to leave his office. "Yes, Susan?"

"You have a visitor. Pilar de los Santos."

Scottie's eyes darkened, and her whole face stiffened.

Bloody hell. What an inopportune moment. Not that he *didn't* want to see Pilar. He did. They were friends. But why was she there?

"Send her back." He disconnected the line.

"Pilar?" Scottie said, repeating the name.

Konrad realized how bad it looked. Women dropping by his office. Scottie had already seen it from day one working for him. He'd felt like such an ass for making her buy gifts for them. By the look on her face, she clearly could not forget it.

"I'm not sure what she wants," he said sheepishly.

"I should go work on the presentation for the EaDo property meeting." She pivoted, but he stopped her.

"No. Stay." Her eyebrows raised. He needed to prove to her he was not the same man. Even if he'd only changed just a little, it was enough. "Come here."

She glanced behind her. "Where?"

"Here." He pointed to himself.

"Someone will see."

"Not if you're quick." The challenge made his heart race, because they could easily be seen. Glass walls. Glass door. They were on display like china. And Scottie looked just as fragile.

She glanced behind her again, walking toward him, slow at first, then faster. Her eyes growing wide and her mouth slightly parting, she seemed unsure of herself. So was he. But he knew one thing. He was going to kiss her. Nothing could stop him, not even the prospect of getting caught.

"Yes," she whispered between heavy breaths.

Konrad glanced outside the glass. No one. He leaned down, taking her bottom lip between his teeth and bit down until she moaned. And just as quickly, he stood, staring at her flushed face.

"You're bad," she said, her fingertips lifting to her mouth.

"I know." He took a step back.

A knock at the door put a mile between them. He took in the curves of Scottie's profile, her lips, her nose, her delicate chin. Where had this woman been all his life?

"Kon?" Pilar's voice took him from his reverie— his dream. His gaze met hers. An odd look washed over her face. She glanced at Scottie. "Is everything okay?"

Scottie answered. "Y-yes."

"Of course. What brings you by?" Konrad asked, accelerating the conversation. As much as he liked Pilar, he didn't like how upset Scottie was.

Pilar pulled something from her handbag, a flash of chrome catching the light. "I found this under my bed. Your watch."

Fuck. Of all the places, it had to be Pilar's apartment, where he'd been many times. Fear slipped into his body, making him tense up. When he looked at

Scottie, she looked like she'd been kicked in the stomach. All her insecurities were on her face again. This was her problem with him. He knew it. And though they'd made strides since Sunday, this might set them back. He could feel it in his bones.

"I'll leave you guys to talk. Excuse me." Scottie left the room faster than he could form another thought. The door snapped closed behind her.

"She was there that night, at your friend's party." Pilar's stare was intense on him, her eyebrows lifted.

He nodded, moving to his chair and sitting heavily in it. "She's my temp. It was a coincidence. I had no idea she would be there."

Pilar walked to a chair across his desk and sat, setting the watch on a stack of folders. She looked up at him, not saying a word, just staring with glossy black eyes. "It's her, no?"

He rubbed the back of his neck, his thoughts on Scottie. What must she be thinking? Feeling? His past had come back to hit her in the face, and he hated it.

"What do you mean?"

She touched her bottom lip, red and full. "You have lipstick here."

He sank back in his chair, rubbing his lips together. "Oh."

"She's why you changed so fast. Right?" Pilar crossed her bare legs.

Yes. "Thank you for bringing my watch. I thought I'd lost it forever."

Pilar laughed. "You're like this watch."

Lost and found. Maybe. That was too simple though. "Pretentious and obscenely expensive? Yes, I'm quite like it."

She shook her head, standing. "Bye, *guapo*."

He waited until she walked to the door, and just

before she opened it, he called to her. "Pilly…"

She turned to him. "*Sí* ?"

"She is why." There. He'd said it. And he meant it.

Pilar nodded, a ghost of a smile on her lips and a sparkle in her eyes. "Good." A second later, she was outside of his office and down the hall.

Scottie hadn't been at her desk, though, when he'd stepped back out in the aisle. His anxiety flared. She'd run again, as she had the times it was too much for her. He wanted her to stop running, to trust him. Let him prove to her what he wanted to prove to himself. But it had to be with his actions, words weren't going to prove anything to either of them.

He found her in the break room. Jeff was at her side, making her laugh, which Konrad hated. He clenched his jaw at the sight, wanting nothing more than to fire Jeff for being alive. *Calm down, Korr.* He needed to contain himself. Scottie had been in his bed last night. She would not walk away so easily.

"Scottie, I need to talk to you." His voice boomed louder than he intended.

She continued to stir her cup of coffee, not looking up at him. "About?"

Jeff's eyes widened. Scottie was too defiant to be professional, but he knew it was her hurt and insecurity talking. Still, he grew angry at her indignation in front of his employees. "Now, Scottie."

"Pardon me, Jeff. Duty calls." She lifted her cup. "And yes, I will have lunch with you today."

Konrad's fists clenched. Why was this her answer? Why did she punish him for a past he wanted to forget? What did she want from him? What did she need from him to get past her fear of him?

He took the coffee cup from her hands and placed

it on the counter as they walked out of the break room. "You won't need that."

"I wanted that!" She'd raised her voice.

"Keep it down, Scottine. This is my office, and you will not cause a scene."

She pressed her lips together, disdain coloring her face. She followed him down the hall and out of the suite. Konrad didn't bother to say a word to Susan, who still chatted with Marisol. *Sod them*. His careless urgency drove him. He'd worry about the consequences later.

He stopped Scottie at the lift and pressed the button to summon the car. He didn't know where they were going, but he needed to get her out of his building. To his surprise, she didn't say another word, only followed him.

Outside, in the unbearable heat, they faced each other. "You're not having lunch with Jeff."

"You left your watch under Pilar's bed. So I think I can have lunch with Jeff."

He shook his head. "I left that watch there before I met you, Scottie. You know who I used to be."

She crossed her arms, turning her face away from the sun. "I know who you *are*."

He grabbed her wrist, pulling her arms apart. He hated the barrier she'd created between them. "Was, Scottie. Who I *was*. I'm not that bloke anymore. If you can't believe me, we don't have a chance."

She yanked away from him. "I guess we don't have a chance then."

He was stunned. After what they'd shared, it was hard to hear those words. He thought they'd agreed to let the past live in the past. "If you believe that, walk away right now."

She shook her head, the turmoil evident on her face. They stared for several beats before she pivoted on her heels away from him, his heart falling. Before he reached for her, she turned, her eyes bright and glossy. "I don't want to."

He didn't touch her. He didn't pick her up like he wanted to do. "Pilar knows about you. So does Dallas. And soon, I want everyone to know you're with me."

He'd barely recognized his words, or his voice. This was not the Konrad he knew and loved. This Konrad was brave despite the fear that kept him dangling on the edge, since he knew his feelings were different with Scottie.

She was shocked. "Oh…"

"What time is the meeting with Ortho-Sync?" Konrad needed to be with her.

"It moved to two this afternoon." Her voice quivered.

"You're coming with me." He took her hand. "I'll have to buy you a new dress after what I have in mind."

She gasped. "You mean it?"

Pulling her toward the parking garage street entrance, he said, "Let me show you how much I mean it."

Chapter Twenty-Six

"Do you think anyone will notice I have on a different dress?" Scottie looked down at the first couture dress she'd ever owned.

"Not a chance." Konrad winked at her from the driver's seat of his sports Mercedes.

"I'll return it tonight." She couldn't imagine keeping the almost thousand-dollar dress. For that reason, she'd not removed the tag.

"Don't be absurd. It's a gift." He turned the wheel to get on Main Street. "After all, I completely ripped your other one. I owed you."

"You didn't owe me." She looked at her unmanicured fingers. "I would have taken the loss."

"You don't have to take a loss with me, *Schatzi*." The words fell from his lips as if they were easy to say.

Was it really that easy now? Though she felt more at ease with him, like she had on Sunday, she still felt sensitive. This was real. It was all becoming more real with each moment with him. She'd always thought her worst fear was she'd fall in love and be completely crushed and abandoned. She'd felt that early on in life. The feeling kept her in a box. Konrad made her want out of that box. But it meant falling, and she was on her way.

"What kind of loss would you take?" What an odd question for her to ask, but she really wanted to know how far he'd go.

He stalled, pensive as he came to a stoplight. "I'm not sure I can answer that."

She stared at the sleek lines of the inside of his car. She knew how much he loved it. It was his identity. "Would you give up this car?"

He laughed. "Not a chance. This is my baby."

"Not even for happiness?"

"This car brings me happiness." He turned to her. "This car and I have been through a lot."

A lot of women. Scottie had to force the thought out of her mind. She'd have to stop it. Or walk away, and walking away was not an option.

"I could give up everything for happiness," she said, sitting back in the plush leather bucket seat. "Happiness is all there is."

He stepped on the gas again when the light turned green. "We should all be so lucky."

She turned to him, taking in his profile. "Well, I feel happy right now. With you. In this car."

He smiled, eyes still on the road. "Good. So do I."

She smiled, turning her gaze forward again. Yes, this was happiness. It had to be. And she felt safe. That might be all she ever wanted.

****

After the meeting with Ortho-Sync, Scottie and Konrad stayed behind in the conference room. Konrad was beaming. It was a done deal. Scottie, however, couldn't forget the Bayou Sling team. True, they were offering five percent below asking price, while the medical device company offered two percent over asking price, but didn't the Bayou Sling deserve a chance? EaDo was perfect for the brewery. They could gain customers quickly and offer tours in the facilities. Plus, Scottie liked their give-back program. They hired veterans and freed convicts who were trying to rehabilitate. And they were a green company, advocates for recycling and minimizing their carbon footprint.

Scottie thought Konrad had made a mistake by only looking at the bottom line. Bayou Sling could offer more for the community than the medical device plant could.

He closed his laptop. "That rooftop patio condo community is as good as mine."

"Another condo community?"

"Of course. Why not?"

She looked down at her hands. "I think Bayou Sling deserves the location."

He frowned. "That's not feasible. I already explained the bottom line to you."

"Bottom line is they will have a more meaningful impact in the long run. This medical device company manufactures artificial hip parts, which is important, but they can put that manufacturing plant anywhere. Bayou Sling can't be just anywhere."

Konrad thought a moment. Then his lips curled. "That's so romantic, Scottie, but I'm a businessman. I make money, and I will make plenty of money with this sale."

She shrugged, knowing it was a lost cause. "I just think if the opportunity for something good comes along, you should take it."

He stood, slipping his laptop under his arm. "Oh, I intend to. With you."

Just like that, her mind was off Bayou Sling. She smiled at him, memories of their morning coming back, sending ripples through her body. "What do you have in mind?"

"Taking you home with me. Feeding you Chinese take away. Then giving you the most intense pleasure you've ever known."

The apex of her thighs throbbed. "Why wait?"

His eyebrows lifted. "Come again?"

"Indeed." She stood, thinking she wanted to taste him. She wanted to give him pleasure as he'd given her. "The copy room is empty." And there was a proper wall and door for privacy.

"You're quite naughty, aren't you?" He grinned.

"Yes." She walked to the glass conference room door and pulled the door handle. "I'll be waiting for you."

Five minutes later, Scottie heard the door of the copy room open. Konrad filled the doorway. God, this man was so beautiful. He closed the door, holding her stare as he locked it.

"You can't make any noise. Not everyone's left for the day yet."

"*My* noise won't be the problem." She gave him a wicked grin.

His eyebrows lifted. "Oh?"

She walked over to him, dropping to her knees in front of him.

"Scottie," he groaned.

"Let me do this. I haven't yet." She unbuckled his belt. "I want to so much."

She'd never necessarily wanted to do that with a man. It had never occurred to her that she could give pleasure. She'd never felt protected enough to want to. But, with Konrad, she'd stay on her knees until they ached to show him how protected she felt.

She unzipped his trousers, pushing down until they pooled at his feet. He gasped at his freed erection as she stroked him. She was in control. No question there. And it was exhilarating to see this big, hard man succumb to her.

Though she'd never done this with a man, she knew by instinct alone what to do. She put him in her mouth, tasting him. Going further, she took him fully in her mouth, her grip tight on his base. He thrust his hands into her ponytail.

"My God, Scottie. Your mouth … it's…" He

groaned. "Heaven."

She continued. Feeling him. Knowing what he wanted her to do. The satisfaction she'd received from this act made her feel free. She'd even forgotten where she was. She just kept pleasuring him until he grew steel hard in her mouth and yanked her ponytail.

"I'm coming," he choked out, and attempted to remove himself from her mouth.

But she remained and took every bit of him, swallowing it down until he stopped, and she became aware of her aching knees.

Scottie sat back on her heels, staring up at him anew. Everything was new in her eyes. "Did you like it?"

He dropped to his knees, pulling her into him. "Fuck yes."

His mouth came down on hers in a savage kiss. She was floating, and she knew this was what people talked about. This feeling. This was true ecstasy. True connection.

She'd given him her trust, and she couldn't feel more vulnerable. Or secure.

Chapter Twenty-Seven

By Wednesday, Konrad was on a fucking cloud. That was the only way to express it. It must have been the same cloud Fabian had been on. Now Konrad didn't blame the poor bastard. He understood it, and he couldn't wait to be with Scottie again. He wanted to tell her things he'd never told anyone, to find out everything about her.

"You've got this goofy look in your eyes, Kon. What's the deal?" asked Dallas, breaking Konrad's daydream. The reality was, they were in Dallas's office at Halman Hotel, waiting on a conference call with Jacob Moreau.

"Have you ever been in love?" Konrad felt like an idiot for asking. "And how fast does something like that happen? Shouldn't it take years?"

Dallas sat back in his executive chair, his brown eyes narrowed. "What's wrong with you?"

Konrad sighed. "I don't know."

"Is it your temp?"

She wasn't just his temp anymore. He grinned, looking down at the hotel specs printout.

"No shit!" Dallas dropped his hand on the desk, getting Konrad's attention. "You're in love with your temp."

"Yes. I don't know. Maybe." Fuck. He was in love. He absolutely was. "How do you know if you are?"

"You start acting like Fabian." Dallas chuckled. "And, it looks like you're there, my friend."

"But I've only known her ten days. Is it even possible? I mean, I've had women on rotation for six months and never felt anything like this for them."

"Well, I guess it's because you were just fucking 'em." Dallas didn't candy-coat anything, which is what

Konrad liked about him. "I mean, just using them. You know what I'm saying."

"Eloquent as ever, Mr. Halman." He sighed. He was not just fucking Scottie. He didn't fuck her. He made love to her, which, as it turned out, was a whole different, more satisfying experience entirely. "I'm not using her, and she's not using me."

"Is she your … girlfriend?" Dallas said with hesitation. It seemed weird coming from his lips. Konrad had never thought someone would ask him that question.

He'd also never thought he'd say he was in love. But here he was. "I want her to be."

"Damn. Well, that's a first." Dallas shook his head in disbelief.

"I can't really do anything about it right now though. Not while she's my temp." How would they get around it? He couldn't request another temp. That would seem as if Scottie was unsuitable. And she wouldn't let him hire her, which probably was for the best. She'd have to get a job elsewhere. "Are you hiring?"

Dallas laughed but stopped when he realized Konrad was dead serious. "In corporate? I'm not sure. Wait … are you seriously asking me?"

Konrad leaned back in his chair. "Not really. It would be so much better if she had a permanent job somewhere."

"Though, does she really need one?" Dallas glanced at his screen following an email notification. "How serious are you about her?"

"I think fairly to moderately." Konrad shook his head. "No, more. Severely serious."

"Well, just move her into your place."

Konrad had already thought of that, but he didn't think it was the time to ask. Something told him she would reject the idea, which he admired. Most women he'd bedded would jump at the chance to be the queen of his penthouse.

The phone rang before Konrad could answer. It was Jacob. Konrad put on his business hat and focused on the hotel he intended to buy. However, the idea of Scottie living in his penthouse didn't leave his mind once.

****

Konrad stayed at Halman Hotel for the rest of Wednesday, discussing the new boutique hotel. He'd felt good about the purchase. They'd agreed to go to Dallas the next day to discuss terms and meet with Jacob's team. A whole day without seeing Scottie would be torture. Because of that, he'd planned a romantic evening as soon as he left Halman.

He took out his phone to send a text.

Me: *Schatzi*—**I'll not be back to the office. But, I'm picking you up at eight tonight for the best night of your life. Thoughts?**

Immediately, she responded.

Scottie: **You know my thoughts.**

He smiled. If she only knew his.

Me: **I do.**

Scottie: **See you at eight.**

"What are you smiling at?" Dallas walked over from his mini bar, two glasses of scotch in each hand.

"Scottie." Konrad took the glass.

"My God. You are in love." He shook his head and drank. "Damn love is taking my friends."

Konrad laughed. "You're next, Dallas. I can feel it."

"Nah. I'll say Tylund is. I swear he and Mel act like an old married couple."

Konrad shook his head. "No. It's you. You're next. I'd bet my Mercedes on it."

"Hmmm. I'll take that bet. I need to add a Mercedes to my collection."

"And if you lose? What do I get?" Konrad took a sip, savoring it.

"To keep your Mercedes."

"That's not fair!" Konrad laughed. "You have to give something up."

Dallas thought a moment, setting down his glass. "I tell you what. If I lose, I'll let you buy me out on the hotel."

"That's a big wager, Dallas." Konrad didn't think Dallas could be serious.

"Love is a big wager."

Indeed.

Chapter Twenty-Eight

Scottie waited in the living room, wearing her little black dress. She'd worn it to her graduation dinner in May, and to an evening out afterward with Tara and a couple other classmates she'd kept in touch with. Not many though.

"I see cleavage. Must be a special night." Tara walked into the living room, her Decadent Chick apron wrapped around her waist, sarcasm twisting her lips.

"You already stated your opinion, Tara. I don't need to hear it again." She glanced at her cell phone. Five until eight. "Where's Brett? Can't you annoy him instead?" That was low. Scottie felt regret immediately after.

"He isn't around anymore. But of course, you wouldn't know because you've been screwing your boss every night this week. I've hardly seen you."

Scottie snapped her eyes to Tara. When had she become so cruel? She'd not remembered their relationship hitting this low in the past twenty years of their friendship.

"God, Tara. It's not like that." Scottie's voice grew soft. "What happened with Brett?"

Tara sighed heavily, her head falling in her palm. "Nothing. I'm sorry. I've been really upset lately."

Scottie didn't know what to say. It wasn't okay for Tara to treat her that way, but she forgave her anyway. "I know you have."

"I need help with another catering job. It's a party for fifty people on Friday. Can you do it?"

The doorbell rang. Scottie didn't inquire about the party. With only a few more hundred dollars before she could buy her brooch back, she couldn't refuse.

Everything was finally starting to fall into place for her. "Yes, I'll do it." The doorbell rang again. "I have to go."

"God, he's demanding. Give a girl a minute to answer the door." Tara rolled her eyes and walked back into the kitchen, her attitude resurfacing.

Scottie sighed, grabbing her clutch and the overnight bag she'd packed, and strode to the door with Konrad on the other side.

His blue eyes gleamed like sapphires. "My God, we may not make it to dinner."

"We better." She slipped outside and closed the door behind her. "I'm starving."

He leaned down to kiss her, his moan dancing in her ear. "Yes, milady."

Like the gentleman she'd started to see him as, Konrad opened the passenger door and helped her in the sports car. "You smell good," he said.

"Thank you." She rode her palms up his chest from his naval, his eyes eating her alive as she did it.

"I thought you were starving? A move like that will get you naked in my bed without dinner."

"Oh…" She dropped her hand in her lap. "Sorry."

He laughed, shutting the door. Scottie watched him walk around the front, all the while thinking how lucky she was. Despite any initial impression, he was perfect. He was an absolute dream. He was *the* dream.

Konrad drove the car through the Heights and into the Museum District to L'Atelier Restaurant. Scottie had never been there. Inside, Konrad had reserved the chef's private table for two, complete with prix fixe menu and wine pairing. Scottie noticed all the attention they received. Konrad couldn't be missed. With his suit and handsome looks, every set of eyes were on him. She'd have to get used to it.

She became aware of Konrad staring at her from

across the table. She'd been too focused on everyone else. "What?" She felt nervous. Aware of herself.

"Do you have any idea how beautiful you are?"

The heat of embarrassment warmed her cheeks. "I-I don't know." Konrad had been the only one to say that to her with that look in his eyes. As if he really meant it.

"You should know, and you should never forget it." He took the prix fixe menu, scanning it casually as if he hadn't just rocked her world with his words.

The waiter came to take drink orders. Konrad ordered scotch, of course, and she ordered a lemon drop martini. He snickered when she ordered it.

When the waiter left, Konrad said, "That's not far off from a fuzzy navel, love."

"Shut up!" She threw a sugar packet at him, which was totally unacceptable for the fine dining restaurant.

He tossed it back at her, which was not what she expected. He was too refined to do it. "You're in *so* much trouble, Scottine Roberts."

"I don't think you know what trouble is, Konrad Korr." She narrowed her gaze.

But playtime was quickly over. He grew serious and pensive.

Scottie wanted to know more. She wanted to know what had moved him so much in that moment. "Where did you go?"

"I just thought about my *Mutter*—mother." His answer was quick, but the explanation was put on hold as the waiter set down their drinks.

"Your first course will come out shortly. Are you on the three-hour dining experience?"

Konrad glanced at Scottie. "Can you make it two?"

The waiter nodded. "Of course." He was gone again.

Scottie took her martini glass, her tongue touching the sugared rim. The sweet liquid eased down her throat. Her gaze was still on Konrad, who also had his gaze on her.

"You're waiting for me to finish, aren't you?"

"Yes. If you want to tell me. It's up to you."

He sipped again, dragging the gulp down. She hung on his every move. "I was noncompliant as a youth. She said to me 'you don't know what trouble is, my son.' *Sie wissen nicht, was das Problem ist mein Sohn.* That was the last time I talked to her. She died not long after."

Her heart clenched up. "Oh."

"Your words … it just reminded me of her."

"Oh no. I'm so sorry. I had no idea."

"It's okay. How could you know?" Konrad dropped his gaze a moment. Scottie didn't believe that for one second. He continued on his own accord, "She overdosed on her medication. That's what I was told."

Oh God. Scottie's eyes welled up. Konrad's mother committed suicide? Maybe intentionally? She wanted to go to him and ease that tortured look off his face.

He drank again, this time draining the glass and leaving nothing but a ball of ice. "She had depression."

"That's awful." She was breathless.

"Yeah, it really is."

"Were you close to her?"

His eyes darkened to almost black. The man looked like he was in agony talking about it. It passed quickly though. She wondered how long he'd been suppressing his feelings about it.

"Not as close as I should have been. My father made sure of that." There was a bitterness in his voice.

Scottie's heart could burst with all the emotions she felt. She didn't blame him anymore for who he was. How could a person get close to someone else when the prospect of losing them was all too possible? Scottie knew the feeling. Her own father might as well have been dead.

"Does your father live in Germany?"

He shook his head, looking done with the heavy stuff. "No. That bastard lives six feet under in Austria." Konrad lifted his glass to their passing waiter.

"I'm sorry. I hope I haven't ruined this evening with my questions." She reached out to touch his hand and get his full attention. "I just wanted to know."

He smiled, weaving his fingers through hers. "I know. That's what I love about you. You want to know me."

She did. She wanted to know everything.

****

Thursday morning arrived too fast. She woke in Konrad's arms, warm and comfortable. She was sore all over from their perfect night. Konrad stirred, pulling her tighter into him, his thick leg slung over her hip. There was no escaping him.

"Kon?" She rubbed his forearm that was crossing her chest. He moaned, nuzzling her neck. His erection hit the back of her thigh, and she wanted him again. "Kon?"

"Mmm … keep doing that, and you'll be late for work," he whispered against her ear.

She pushed herself farther into his erection. Before she knew it, he awoke, gripping her hips, his erection moving against her, back and forth, teasing her. Reminding her how powerful he was.

She moaned in pleasure. Every cell in her body sparked with energy. She wanted him so much. Every morning, she wanted to wake up this way.

He groaned as he pushed inside of her, filling her, making her soreness pop. "You feel so amazing. I don't think I'll ever tire of this."

She thrust her hips back into him, finding a rhythm that took her to the edge. They were moving together, like an orchestra, feeling each other, hearing each other, knowing each other as they reached their heights of pleasure.

"Yeah," he moaned, his lips on her shoulder, sucking her skin. "Do you like it?"

"I love it," she cried, taking his faster, harder thrusts. She begged for them.

"I want this all the time, Scottie," he said, breathless between movements. "I want you like this every morning."

"What?" she choked out, moving harder against him.

"You and me." He went faster still, making her pinnacle of pleasure emerge quickly. "I want you to be my girlfriend."

In a hard explosion within, she came undone. The room fell around her, and she was falling into Konrad. He was next, pulling her into him as he pulled out of her and released against her. His heart beat wildly through his skin. She could count every pulse. It matched hers.

When she'd calmed, resuming normal breathing, she turned to face him. His eyes were closed, and he looked peaceful. "Konrad?"

Slowly opening his eyes, he gave her those gorgeous ocean eyes that made her heart still. "Yes, baby."

"I want that too. I want to be your girlfriend."

He kissed her softly, then hard. When they parted, she couldn't imagine him being the man she'd met less than two weeks ago. Had it only it been eleven days? It felt more like eleven months. Eleven years.

"I always thought, if my father didn't want to hang around, why would anyone else? But you changed that for me. You changed me." She closed her eyes because she didn't want to cry.

Warm fingertips trailed down her cheek. Konrad kissed her fallen tear. "And you changed me too, *Schatzi*."

****

Konrad dropped off Scottie at the office just after nine in the morning. He'd summoned his pilot to fly his company plane to Dallas for a meeting and would be gone all day. Scottie kissed him before she opened the car door.

"I'll be back later today."

"Okay."

"You're coming with me to guys' night this evening. I want to introduce you properly."

"But this job…"

"Don't worry. We'll work it out." He caressed her cheek. The man could be so tender.

Scottie nodded. Yes, they would work it out somehow. In the meantime, she intended to look for permanent work on her own. Without the agency.

"Bye." She slipped out of the car.

"Cheerio, babe."

She closed the door, watching him speed away in his chick magnet. Sighing, she turned toward the Korr Corp building. She was beyond late. She hoped no one would ask any questions.

Inside, she walked through the lobby, Susan waving at her. Thank goodness she'd been on a call, as usual. But she called to her just before Scottie walked into the suite.

"Scottie…"

"Yes?"

Susan pulled out a garment bag and handed it over the reception desk. "Konrad's dry cleaning was delivered."

"Oh … okay." She took the heavy garment bag, which had been several suits on hangers banded together. "Thanks."

In Konrad's office, she hung the garments on a rolling rack he had near his mini bar while she called Space City Pawn on her cell phone. A man answered on the first ring.

"Space City Pawn."

Scottie held the phone up to her ear with her shoulder as she straightened the bags, removing the band that connected the hangers. "Hi, I'm calling about an item I pawned last week."

"Which item?" He seemed bored.

"A Rene Lalique gold brooch. You gave me twelve hundred for it." Just as she shook the last bag containing a suit jacket, a Post-it attached to a folded napkin fell off.

"Oh right," he said. A rustle of papers filled the receiver.

Scottie bent over to pick up the folded napkin. "Is it still available?"

"Yeah."

Scottie scanned the print on the Post-it. *Found in pocket.* Scottie frowned. "You said I can get it back for what I sold it for."

"No." His tone was harsh. "That's a twenty-four-hour option. It's been a week. The price is five thousand now. I've already had a couple of interested buyers. So, I can't guarantee the price won't go up."

Her heart stopped. *No.* "What?" To stall herself from the real prospect that she would never see her grandmother's brooch again, she opened the attached napkin, quickly wishing she had not.

"Sorry, ma'am. But you signed the contract of sale."

The napkin was filled with Konrad's handwriting. She'd recognize it anywhere. She dropped her phone, and read the words again.

September Hookups
H Bar Bartendress
Tamsin
Anisette
Hot Yoga Instructor
Pilar
Greek Starbucks Barista on West Gray Ave.
Temp S.R.

Oh, God. She was Temp S.R., the seventh hookup for this month. It was only the fourteenth of September. Just two weeks into the month. Scottie felt like she'd been run over. Run over and then minced and then dumped on Galveston Beach.

This was the man she was with? This was the man she'd lowered her guard for? This man, who she swore she was falling for, had a hookup list for September. And she was *seventh* on it. How many more were there? God. She didn't want to know.

The tears fell. Her heart fell. And she would have fallen on her knees if the damn walls and doors weren't glass. In anger, she stormed to his desk, ripping a piece of tape from the dispenser. She took the napkin and taped it to the seat of his pretentious executive chair. He wouldn't miss it there. That should give him all the explanation he needed when she wasn't in her cube when he returned. Ever.

She stormed to her desk, retrieving her purse. She never wanted to see the inside of Korr Corp ever again.

Or the Korr penthouse. She was done.

Chapter Twenty-Nine

Life was good. After a great meeting with Jacob Moreau, the contract to purchase basically signed, Konrad was ready to get back to Houston. He'd told Dallas he intended to bring a surprise guest to guys' nights. Scottie and his relationship would be in the open. To his circle at least, which was the only thing that mattered to him.

The job situation would have to be handled with delicate precision. Scottie would get a permanent job and leave on her own accord, hopefully in no more than two weeks. No one would have to know the real reason. Then, when enough time had passed, he'd tell the whole world she was his.

These thoughts exhilarated him. This plan he'd thought up made him step harder on the gas pedal. He needed to get to her. Fast.

He parked in his prime parking spot and flipped down the visor to take a look at himself. He met his own gaze. Blue and intense. His straight nose. Had he always looked so much like his mother? The conversation he'd had with Scottie about his mother was hard. That part of his life had always been hidden. No one really knew what had happened with her—the overdose, the suicide. The neglectful husband and father who saw family as a burden. He'd avoided facing the truth because it had always been too painful.

He stared harder into his eyes. With Scottie, he could face himself. Finally. And she wouldn't run away. After hearing about his mother and still not running away … she was the real deal. And knowing who he was before, the player. The noncommittal guy who kept his distance because being close was scary. Nothing he could tell her would make her leave him. Abandon him. He couldn't survive her abandonment, not where his heart was concerned.

He pulled out his phone, a smile on his face. God, he loved her.

Me: I'm coming for you. I hope you're ready for me.

He laughed at his text. She was his, bottom line. And after today, his closest friends, who were his only family, would know about her. Pride filled him. Scottie was the best thing that had ever happened to him.

He got out of his car, half wondering why he'd not received a text back. He glanced at his Richard Mille watch. Only half past four. She should be at her cube. He frowned, turning to face the VIP parking spot he'd given her. And…

No car. Scottie wasn't there.

His heart raced and so did he as he moved quickly inside the building and into the lift. Several people stopped to chat with him. A woman who'd been eyeing him since her company leased a suite from Korr Properties tried to chat him up. But, he couldn't think straight.

In the Korr Properties suite, he went to Scottie's cube. Empty. Where the hell was she? He walked back to reception. Susan had been flipping through a magazine. The phones usually died down around that time.

"Konrad!" She was surprised. "You look … scared."

"Where's Scottie?" he demanded, making her jump.

"Uhh … I … she left this morning." Her eyes were wide, scared. "Said she didn't feel well. I called the temp agency, and they offered to send someone for today. I told them no since you were out. Was that okay?"

"I didn't know she was ill." He pulled his cell phone out again from his suit jacket pocket and called her. Still, no response.

Konrad calmed some though. If she was ill, then she must be sleeping. Something felt wrong. Without responding to Susan, he pivoted on his heels and remerged into the suite. With unsteady hands, he poured himself a glass of scotch. He drained it and quickly poured himself another.

One of his accountants stood at his door. He shook his head. "Not now."

She frowned. "But I—"

"I said not now." He opened his door, letting it close behind him.

His heart raced a thousand beats per second. Scanning his office, he felt cold. Weird, since it had been the end-of-summer heat. He usually felt warm in the office.

Walking to his mini bar, he noticed his dry cleaning was hanging on the garment rack he kept for extra dress shirts. Nothing seemed unusual there.

His phone vibrating in his pocket made him jump. Elation took him. Scottie! He pulled the phone from his pocket again. Not Scottie.

Fabian P: **Heard you're bringing a guest to guys' night? Spill it, Korr.**

Fuck! He put the phone on the bar, scrubbing his face. God, he needed to calm down. He should sit. Get his bearings. Scottie had to be home in bed. Where else could she possibly be?

As he walked to his desk, he saw his chair had been pushed under the desk. He yanked it out from under the desk and saw the hookup list he'd written taped to the seat. *Oh, God, no.* His heart stopped. The glass of scotch fell from his grip, crashing to the floor and shattering.

No. No. No. No.

He snatched the list from the chair, lifting it to his eye line. Scottie had seen it. Scottie had found this. She'd read it. She knew who Temp S.R. was. The worse thing that could have happened, happened.

He turned toward the dry cleaning hanging on the rack. Could she have found the napkin in the dry cleaning? Konrad thought the napkin was long gone— not waiting in the shadows for him to be happy, only to pounce and ruin his life.

If Scottie believed this list, believed she was just another on a list, she would never forgive him. He crushed the napkin in his palm. Weren't they past that? For the first time in his life, he wanted to cry. He wanted to weep for tasting happiness and then maybe losing it.

What could he do to correct this? In the only way Konrad knew how to make things better, he stormed out of his office, leaving everyone in his wake to stare, and jumped in his car. First stop, Space City Pawn.

Chapter Thirty

"He's not leaving, Scott." Tara peered through the peephole. "He looks pretty messed up."

"Good." Scottie's jaw clenched. She'd fought through sadness the whole day, and finally she'd gotten mad. Livid. *Number fucking seven!* "He deserves it."

"I told you not to get involved with him."

"Save it," Scottie snapped. She wasn't in the mood to take any shit.

Tara turned to face her, her cheeks red. "You're right. Sorry." She turned her attention to the peephole.

Konrad knocked on the door. Was he drunk? His muffled words came through the door. "Scottie, please open the door. I need to talk to you. Explain."

"There's nothing to explain," Scottie yelled from the living room.

"He probably can't hear you."

"Shut up, Tara." Scottie raked her fingers through her wild waves.

Tara faced the door again, her hand gripping the doorknob. She turned it, opening it just a sliver.

Scottie couldn't see him, though she stupidly wanted to.

"She doesn't want to talk to you, Konrad," said Tara.

The sadness came back. The devastation. The insecurity. The pain of the lie. She believed Konrad could be different than what he was. He'd made a great claim. He'd hooked her. He'd made her believe she was the one exception, but she was no exception. Konrad couldn't change. He had too much baggage to let himself be vulnerable, and she was just a fool with a dream.

A fool with a broken heart.

"Please, tell her. Tell her to come outside. Talk to me for five minutes. One minute. That's all I ask."

Scottie could almost hear him breathe.

"Just a single minute," he said, his voice full of anguish.

Against her better judgment, Scottie walked across the living room and opened the door wider until Konrad came into view. Tara was right. He looked completely messed up. Her heart clenched, but, she held back the tears and the urge to comfort him. Who would comfort her, dammit?

"Are you sure?" Tara's voice was muffled to Scottie's ears.

Scottie's attention was on her own heart beating and Konrad's glowing blue eyes, rimmed with red. "Yeah." She stepped outside, closing the door behind her.

Konrad embraced her, but she shoved him away. "No, Konrad. You can't touch me."

He closed his eyes, shaking his head. "It was stupid. You shouldn't have ever seen that list."

Her heart throbbed, the tears fighting her to fall, but she refused. "Clearly." She crossed her arms.

"It doesn't mean anything. It was from before."

"It was a fucking hookup list. For September, Konrad. September!" The anger bubbled up inside her, exploding with her words.

He dropped his head. "I know…"

"When did you write that list?" She needed to know, though the answer would hurt her worse.

He shook his head, sighing. "I don't remember."
"Bullshit!"

His eyes snapped to hers.

Scottie silently dared him to be angry. He had no right.

Standing straighter, he said, "After we got together."

"You mean after we fucked in your office the first time?" She was being crude because the hurt had taken over.

"Don't say that." His voice was low, pained.

"When?"

He shrugged. "The day after that. Friday. It was a stupid thing we did."

"Who?"

"Dallas and I."

The wind was knocked out of her. "Wait. You two compared your hookups lists? Are you serious, Konrad?"

He nodded.

In a low voice, more controlled than she'd been thus far, she asked, "Who had the most hookups? You or Dallas?"

"Scottie, this doesn't matter. It was before. I want *you*. I'm with *you*," he said, a plea in his voice.

"You or Dallas?"

Silence.

She stared at him hard. She wanted to see every inflection, every flinch. She wanted to see the truth in his eyes. And she was so close to being devastated, she was shaking.

Konrad shook his head, his gaze lifting to the sky. When he looked back at her, his face was white as a ghost. "Me."

The tears fell. Hard. Scottie didn't know how to console herself. She'd never faced anything like this. Lifting her hands to her face, she cried in her palms.

"Baby," Konrad pleaded, taking her in his arms. She let him because she couldn't fight him. She was too weak. He kissed her hair and held her like his life depended on it. "Please, don't cry. Please…"

She pushed him away finally and put several feet between them.

Going to her, he pulled something from his pocket. "Scottie, I want to make it right. I want you to forgive me. Please."

He thrust a box in her hand. Thoughts spun in her mind. She could barely stay upright. She held the box in her hand as if it was an object she'd never seen before. Her watery gaze lifted to meet his.

"Open it." He seemed hopeful.

Curiosity alone made her open it, and she'd wished she hadn't. Inside was the reason she had to walk away. It was her grandmother's brooch, the one she'd asked him not to buy back for her. Anger rushed through her, fueling her.

"No!" She threw the box at him. "You can't buy me, Konrad! You can't get me back with things! Throwing money at me won't make me turn a blind eye to your little trysts. Not even my grandmother's brooch can do that. Get out of here."

His eyes grew wide. "What?"

"Leave." She was trembling so hard her knees knocked. "I don't want to see you."

"But." He retrieved the box from the concrete and held out it out to her. "I … want to work this out."

"You're not going to change. You don't want to. Maybe you can't." She steadied herself, knowing she would never see her grandmother's brooch again. "And I can't trust you. I don't trust I will always be the only one for you."

"But you are."

"Until when? You see the next hot barista on West Gray Avenue?" Her voice hardened.

"Scottie…"

"It's over." The tears came fast, her heart in her throat. She had to walk away from him. It was the only option.

Chapter Thirty-One

"I see…" Konrad didn't know how to have a conversation about Scottie with A-Plus Temporaries. He didn't take personnel-type calls. But this was *personal*. He wanted to know where she was. What she was doing.

"We do expect our temporaries to seek permanent employment, but usually they finish assignments, so I apologize for the abrupt departure of Scottine Roberts. I am more than happy to send a replacement today for the duration of the contract."

Bloody hell. Three months was a long time for someone else to sit across from him. Take his notes. Schedule his appointments. He knew Scottie would eventually get another job, but this was not how he had envisioned it happening.

"Of course. But no worries for today. Send the new temp on Monday." He needed to get off the call.

"No problem, Mr. Korr. We'll send a suitable temp on Monday morning."

"Thank you."

"Thank you, sir. Have a wonderful day."

"You as well." He hung up, a sigh blowing out of him the size of Eastern Europe.

Konrad stared at his computer screen. No way did Scottie get another job so fast. They'd only broken up last night. There was no job available that quickly. It was clear Scottie had left the contract and, from the sound of it, left the agency.

His phone buzzed, taking him from his thoughts and a little bit from the misery of not having her. It was Fabian.

Fabian P: **You missed guys' night. You better NOT miss tonight.**

Another fucking get-together with those two? Hadn't they had enough celebrating? *Bloody-fucking-hell*. They acted like they were the only couple who'd ever decided to marry. Yes, Konrad was feeling bitter and tender from his wounds—because he felt indescribably wounded.

Me: **We'll see.**

Fabian P: **Come on, man. A guy turns twenty-nine only once.**

Oh right. It was Konrad's birthday too. He usually enjoyed celebrating, but that year he had no desire to celebrate if Scottie wouldn't be by his side.

Me: **I don't want to make a big deal of it.**

Fabian P: **Nah. Just us guys having a drink at Antonia's. She'll be out with Mel tonight.**

Well, at least it wasn't another engagement dinner. Konrad squeezed the bridge of his nose. He groaned, not wanting to go. The best thing he could think about doing was falling face first into his bed. His lonely, cold bed that Scottie should be in.

Me: **Fine.**

Fabian P: **Excellent!**

Konrad already regretted it. He liked being social, but he just wanted to be himself. Be bummed. Be emotional. Be "off" for once.

The loud buzz of his intercom jolted him to attention. He'd been lost in his thoughts.

"Konrad?" Susan's voice called through the speaker.

"Yes?" He glanced back at his email. The contract for the EaDo property sale to the Ortho-Sync company popped up.

"Mr. Halman is here to see you."

Konrad skimmed over the email. "Send him back."

He sat back, thinking about the EaDo sale. For some reason, he thought of what Scottie had said about the Bayou Sling. *If the opportunity for something good comes along, you should take it.*

A knock on the door grabbed his attention. Dallas waited at the door, coming in when Konrad waved him in.

"Hey." Dallas walked over to the desk, taking Konrad's hand in their usual greeting handshake and pat on the back. He sat. "Happy birthday, old man."

"Piss off!" Konrad chuckled, as did Dallas. "And thank you."

"How you holding up?"

"How do I look like I'm holding up?" Konrad knew he'd seen better days. He was actually wearing a plain white t-shirt and ripped jeans today, much more casual than normal. A suit had felt too constricting, too daunting to wear.

Dallas looked Konrad over. "Well, you've looked prettier."

Konrad laughed. "I feel like absolute ass."

"Yeah … you look like it too. Sorry to break it to you."

Konrad laughed again, pitifully. He was silent, getting his thoughts together. "Thanks for taking my call last night, mate. I thought I was going mad. I've never felt like that before. I can't say I like it much." He'd seen other men grovel. Heard of it. Never had done it himself. But, the thing was, he'd do it again for the right reason. The right person.

"Ah, no problem, Kon. That's what bros are for."

"Indeed."

Dallas had had his head on straight last night. At least one of them had. Konrad had been fit to be tied, as Dallas would say.

"So, what are you gonna do?"

Konrad sighed, leaning back in his chair. There was only one thing to do. "Get her back. I don't know how, but I have to. It's the only thing I know for sure."

"I kinda feel like it's my fault, really. I mean, I was the one who made you write that list." Dallas creased his forehead.

Konrad shook his head. "It's not about the list. It's the fact that I had a list to write in the first place."

"Are you gonna tell the guys? About Scottie?"

"Not until she's mine again."

Dallas breathed in, scratching the stubble on his chin. "Did she come in today?"

"No. The agency called me and said she'd taken a permanent job somewhere. A new temp is starting on Monday."

Dallas laughed. "Ah, hell, you better not get any ideas with this one."

Konrad stared Dallas square in the eyes. "I'll get Scottie back. And when I do, I'll never let her go."

****

Konrad made himself get dressed for his low-key birthday drink with the guys. He'd replaced the t-shirt with a chambray button-up, sleeves rolled to his elbows, and a proper pair of jeans. Not ripped. He'd also replaced his sneakers with a pair of Prada loafers. Outside, he was Konrad again. Inside, he was forever changed.

Fabian had told him to arrive at eight thirty, which he had. Actually, he was right on the dot. Not unusual for him. Konrad was usually punctual. The front desk let him up to the penthouse easily, unlocking the private lift for him. He sighed as it took him to the top of the high-rise. *I don't want to be here.* He still wanted to be facedown on his bed.

He rang the doorbell, listening for footsteps.

None came. He frowned, knocking hard instead. Perhaps the doorbell wasn't working. Three knocks later, he heard heavy steps against the floor. The door opened, nothing but darkness inside. A rush of dread came over him. He knew what this was.

And out of the darkness came a unanimous cry. "Surprise!" The lights came on, and nearly every person he knew in Houston beamed at him, holding drinks in the air.

Fuck. It was a surprise birthday party.

Chapter Thirty-Two

"I can't believe you didn't tell me this was Konrad's surprise birthday party!" Scottie felt the anxiety turn her stomach. "Are you kidding me, Tara! After last night?" Scottie could kill Tara. She could shove her in the oven with those damn salmon puffs.

Tara's eyes were wide in panic. She'd been dressing a frisée and watermelon salad. "I'm sorry. I really needed someone. I didn't know—"

"That's really fucked up. Tara!" Scottie wanted to walk out on her friend. For real. She'd felt betrayed yet again.

"I'm sorry. I just thought you still needed extra cash."

She dropped her face in her hands. "I don't need to make extra money to buy back the brooch anymore." Scottie really hated her life at the moment. Especially since she still had feelings for Konrad. She hated that last night had happened. Hated more that she couldn't be walking into the party on his arm.

Tara lifted her tongs from the salad. "Wait. What do you mean you don't need to buy the brooch back?"

A minor detail she'd left out from her meltdown after Konrad had left. She sighed. "He bought the brooch for me last night, but I couldn't accept it."

"Are you serious?" Tara was in disbelief. "That's your grandmother's brooch. You cherish that thing. And you didn't accept it from Konrad? Why?"

Scottie stared at her friend. Did Tara really think she was the crazy one? The look in her eyes made it seem that way. "Because he buys everything and everyone. I can't be bought."

Tara stood, stunned. "Wow. I'm not sure who I

feel sorrier for."

Scottie felt like she was punched in the stomach. "I can't believe you said that. And you're still the wrong one here. You used me." She untied her apron. "I'm out of here."

"I know. I'm sorry. I need you, Scottie." Tara's voice was weak. Desperate. "I don't have anyone else."

Scottie closed her eyes, all the memories of their long friendship coming forth. *God.* She could not abandon her friend. There were at least fifty people to serve. Tara couldn't do it alone. But could Scottie swallow her pride? Could she see Konrad, the man who had broken her heart, and serve him and his friends salmon puffs and frisée salad?

Under her breath, she said, "I'm going to regret this." To Tara, she didn't say anything, only retrieved the apron and tied it around her waist again.

"I love you," Tara said, going back to her salad.

"If this isn't love, I don't know what is." Scottie turned to the oven and removed a pan of salmon puffs to plate and serve. Maybe she could put a paper bag over her face. Or maybe she could just be an adult and know sometimes things don't go as planned.

With tray in hand and her heart in her throat, Scottie walked out into the packed penthouse. Through the dining area, the lounging area, and the main living, she hadn't seen Konrad, though she knew he was there. The cheers of his arrival had made her stomach drop to the floor, her anxiety rushing through her like vomit the morning after a binge.

The party was lively. Chatter. Glasses clanking. Laughter. Carefree. It made her both angry and sad. Her stomach flopped again the farther she moved through the maze of beautiful, wealthy people. *I don't want to be here.* Damn her loyalty and love for Tara.

"Salmon puff?" she asked random people, practically thrusting the tray in their faces. She didn't want to see anyone. She was lucky most took one without any conversation, and she slowly grew to hate them and what they represented: her failed attempt at a relationship. Her failed attempt to let someone in.

"Salmon puff?" She raised her gaze to Dallas. Her muscles tensed, her skin burning. *Asshole*. He wasn't, though. Konrad was the asshole. She didn't want to acknowledge the part of her that disagreed with that conclusion. It was all too fresh to take a different perspective.

"Sure, Scottie. I'll take one." He accepted the cocktail napkin she handed him and slid a puff off the tray. He didn't eat it though. Instead, he stared with his brown eyes intense on her, as if he had something to say.

What could *he* possibly have to say? Scottie knew Dallas had known about them, which meant he most certainly knew about last night.

Unnerved, she asked, "Is something wrong with your salmon puff?"

Just walk away, Scottie. She didn't need to hear anything Dallas had to say. And, frankly, she had nothing to say to Dallas. Or to any of Konrad's friends for that matter. She caught gazes with Pilar, who walked a few feet behind Dallas.

Great. Could it get any worse? Scottie definitely had nothing to say to her, but she couldn't help notice how perfect she looked traipsing across the room with her perfect dress and perfect body. Scottie couldn't stop thinking how Konrad knew Pilar. Knew what she looked like naked, and what she sounded like. The thought made her sick. Oh God, was Pilar there with him? No. No. No. Scottie couldn't continue the thought.

"Are you all right?" Dallas asked, his voice

startling her.

"You better eat that before it gets too cold to enjoy." Scottie pivoted, feeling icy cold inside.

"Scottie?" Her name on his lips stopped her. "That list was my fault."

Her heart stopped. Turning, she faced him. "What?"

"I was being an idiot. It was my idea, not his. Don't blame Konrad. He didn't want to do it." Dallas shoved the salmon puff in his mouth.

Breathing in deep, Scottie found her words. "You can't make Konrad do anything."

Dallas gave her a pitiful look, though that could have been her imagination. "No, I can't make him do anything. But you can."

He left her standing there, hanging on to the tray with white-knuckled force. What the hell did that mean? No, she couldn't make Konrad do anything. She was stunned and completely paralyzed. Was she wrong about this?

No, she couldn't be. The list. She'd have to remember the list. It was proof he would not give up anything for her, even after she'd given him every part of her—her loyalty, her vulnerability, her trust. She'd given him everything, despite the fear she had about falling. And he had given her nothing.

"Scottine." The voice was low and deep. And accented. She knew exactly who was attached to that voice.

Don't turn around. Don't ruin Tara's chance to ever get another catering job.

If she turned and faced him, it would be over. All that was inside her would rush out, and she wouldn't be able to stop it.

"Scottie, can you look at me?"

Her intention was to walk away, but she couldn't. Just being near him made her stay. "No."

"Can we please talk?"

"No." She choked on that one word. That one tiny word that meant so much. It was so final. It hurt too much to say anything else, especially when she kept envisioning the list that embodied who Konrad was. *Hot Yoga Instructor at gym. H Bar Bartendress.* She grew angry. Fuming.

"There you are, *guapo*!" The other accented voice Scottie knew came from behind her. Number five on his list.

How could he parade his list in front of her? Scottie felt sick.

"Oh, hey." Konrad greeted Pilar with all the politeness that Scottie knew he had. He was too fucking polite. And when the smack of lips sounded in Scottie's ear, she wanted to die.

This was too much.

She spun on her black Converse, shoving the tray into Konrad's chest. "Salmon puff?"

Pilar's eyes grew wide. "Oh, *mierda*."

"You might want to wipe that lipstick off your face," Scottie barked, feeling completely insane and much too self-aware.

Enough.

Scottie released the tray, letting it drop to the tiled floor. Storming away, she ignored his calls to her. Ignored that the only thing she wanted to do was go to him.

Chapter Thirty-Three

Konrad didn't quite catch the tray. Salmon puffs went flying. God, she really was the worst server.

"*Dios mio, guapo*. She's really mad," Pilar said, kicking a puff with her Louboutins. "What did you do?"

"I'm quite tired of salmon puffs anyhow." Konrad looked up from the mess. Antonia was in his face almost instantly. She'd seen the exchange.

"What happened?" Antonia's dark eyes were intense on him.

"So sorry, Antonia. It was my fault. I accidentally knocked the tray out of Scottie's hands." He rubbed the back of his head. He couldn't let Scottie get too far ahead. Or leave.

Antonia's gaze narrowed further. "You've become quite clumsy around her, Konrad."

The mimosa incident came to mind.

"She's not just your temp, is she?" Antonia waved her hand to someone, whom Konrad assumed was Mary, her housekeeper.

Damn. He needed to come clean about Scottie. He needed to prove himself. He needed to show how far he would go.

"Pardon me." He went for Scottie, following the back of her head through the maze of people, and soon he was behind her. Close enough to smell her sweet perfume. "Scottine!" He called. Or yelled was more like it. She stopped. Everyone did. The reservoir of emotions he'd repressed had opened. Nothing could close it now. "You owe me."

Everything was in slow motion, his heartbeat, his breath.

Scottie turned slowly, as if she pulled the wrath

of hell with her. "Excuse me?"

She dragged out those words, her teeth snarling. Still, she was so beautiful. His heart ached with how beautiful she was. How much he knew she could change his whole life with one decision.

"What do I have to do?"

"Konrad—"

"No. You owe me a chance." Throwing up his hands, he felt the weight of exasperation. The room filled with friends and acquaintances fell away. Scottie was the only one he saw. "You gave me none."

She gasped, shaking her head. Anger colored her cheeks red. Emotions were running high. But this was how he wanted to show her he was serious.

"I said everything last night." Her voice low and contained, she continued, "I have nothing else to say."

"There is a lot more to say." He was quite frantic, completely out of his body. "Tell me what you want. I can give you anything you want."

Regret of the public display would have to come later. He glanced down at his wrist, the Richard Mille watch Pilar returned to him glaring at him. He took it off.

"Here. I'll give up my favorite watch." He tossed it toward a champagne glass sitting on the edge of a nearby table. It missed, falling to the floor, along with the champagne.

Scottie's watery gaze moved over the mess and then met his. His heart skipped. She said nothing, made no indication that she understood what giving up his watch meant.

"Fine. How about my Mercedes? I'll give that up." He dug his hand in his pocket, searching for his keys. Spotting a cringing Dallas through the haze of his madness, he tossed the keys at him. "Here, mate. It's all yours."

"You don't get it." Scottie said, the extent of her pain coming forth with a few tears. "Those are things. I don't want things."

He advanced to her, taking the window of opportunity to finally connect with her again. "Then what? What do you want?" He may as well have crawled to her.

She stepped back from him. "Your loyalty."

The room was silent.

"You have it." He wanted to touch her, to wipe the tears from her face. And kiss her. God, he needed to kiss her.

She wiped her face. "Loyalty is too big a price for you."

His heart slowed down. "What are you saying?"

"What I said last night. It's over."

The room became clear. Everyone came into sharp focus again. He saw everything, everyone. And himself. He'd lost her. Tara pulled Scottie into her side, and Konrad watched his heart walk away.

****

The party was over. Konrad shook his head. Worst birthday in history. It was over. Completely over. He was numb with the realization. Or maybe it was the half bottle of Mortlach he'd drunk as he sat in his office. He couldn't go home or anywhere anyone would look for him.

The events ran through his mind obsessively. Everything thing he said. Everything she said. Everything he wanted to say. Everything he wanted her to say. This should have put him off the desire to be committed to someone, but, it didn't. It made him more determined to feel. To have the experience. Because he'd gotten a glimpse of how good it could be, and he wanted to try.

If not Scottie, then who? He'd not think about that.

He took another drink, feeling buzzed, but at least he'd stopped weeping. He'd only wept once in his life. He'd been sixteen then, and his mother had just died in a hospital. He'd learned about it because his father's secretary had called him at boarding school.

He touched his keyboard, and the computer lit up immediately. He'd not shut down his email, which was unusual. This whole day had been unusual.

At the top of his flagged emails was the contract for the EaDo property. He'd not sent it over to Ortho-Sync as he intended to before the day was over.

The day he'd taken Scottie there came back to him. They'd been strangers then, but he'd known instinctively she'd affect him in some way. And then he thought of what she'd said after the meeting with Ortho-Sync.

He leaned back in his chair. Maybe he had it all wrong. Maybe some things weren't meant to be profited from. He'd only understood profit from a young age and nothing more. Profit was all there was.

He glanced back at the email and, for once, he understood there was something more.

Chapter Thirty-Four

Scottie stayed in bed all Saturday crying. Wailing, actually. Tara could have easily mistaken her for giving birth. Yeah, it was pretty pathetic, but her heart was broken. It had never been broken before, not like this. Not by a man she loved. The one man she'd loved without loyalty was her father, and that hadn't fared well her whole life.

But she'd been so close. She'd seen what it was like to fall for someone. The high was so sweet and vast. The low, on the other hand, was pure devastation. She wanted so much to experience the high again, but that meant the low would always be a possibility.

A knock at her bedroom door took her from her thoughts. She wiped her face against her soggy pillow, moist with tears and snot from her crying sessions.

"Scott?" Tara opened the door. "Are you okay?"

"Yes." She cried again, hugging her pillow. God, she needed to stop this. It wasn't like she'd lost her life. Well, it kind of was that way, in a dramatic sense.

"Oh, Scottie." Tara went to her and sat on her bed. She patted Scottie's back. "Why are you doing this?"

"What do you mean?" She peered up at Tara from the pillow.

"Torturing yourself."

"I'm getting over a breakup." She wiped her eyes and sat up. "This really sucks. I've never done this before."

"Yeah. Breakups suck," said Tara. She shook her head, and Scottie remembered she'd broken up with Brett a week ago.

"I guess we're in the same boat," said Scottie.

She stared at her friend, who seemed totally okay. "How are you handling it so well?"

"Because Brett is a complete jackass." Tara's forehead creased, her lips pressed together in a line.

Scottie crossed her arms over her chest. "Why are men such jackasses?"

"They aren't." Tara leaned back on her arm, rubbing her stomach.

Scottie scoffed. "Name one." Would she ever meet a man who wanted to stay? Who wanted to be loyal and not sleep around? Did that man even exist?

"Konrad."

Her eyes snapped to Tara's, who was not going to retract her statement. "Umm. What?"

"Konrad is not a jackass." Tara lifted her eyebrows. "I kind of think you're the jackass in this scenario."

Scottie felt like her friend had hit her in the face with a dodge ball. "Excuse me? Did you not pay attention? Did you not understand I was seventh on a hookup list for September?"

"Yeah, yeah. I know. You were seventh. I heard." Tara rolled her eyes. What had gotten into her? Scottie didn't know whether to kick her out in anger or cry more.

This wasn't fair. None of it.

"He's a player. You were right." Scottie's temperature rose. "And now you're saying this? What the hell?"

Tara shrugged. "I cringed to see that man beg you for forgiveness."

"As he should!" Scottie wasn't wrong here.

"No." She shook her head. "He didn't have to do any of it. Come over. Beg you at our door. Offer you your grandmother's brooch and then basically get on his hands and knees and beg again at his own surprise birthday party—in front of his friends, no less."

Scottie dropped her gaze to her pillow. She couldn't look at Tara. She couldn't allow herself to see it from that perspective. He had bared himself. Painfully. And she had rejected him harshly. But she'd been hurt, devastated. What else could she have done to protect herself?

"Do you have any idea how many men would say 'oh, well' and move on without another thought?" asked Tara. She glanced at her hand. "Do you know how many men would ghost out, never to be heard from again?"

Scottie knew this from some extent by watching her mother's struggles. There were times her mother had been too depressed to cook because of a breakup. Why wouldn't Scottie want to stay alone after witnessing her mother's pain?

"I don't think I know a guy who would give up a Mercedes for me, Scottie."

Scottie wanted to cry again.

"I know it's hard for you, because of your jackass dad who basically abandoned you, but Konrad isn't him. He didn't abandon you. I think you abandoned him."

But it hurt too much, and Scottie was so scared to admit she might have been wrong. What if he ultimately couldn't be loyal? Could she really take that chance again with him?

"Look…" Tara sighed. "I'm only telling you this because I know what it's like to have no loyalty from a man. I know what it's like to be in love and be a slave to that love and to wonder if he feels the same. But you … you didn't have to worry about that. Konrad is in love with you. Everyone in that room could see it. I don't think any of us can say that wasn't love. I know I can't."

Oh, God. Scottie brought her hands to her face, sighing heavily in them.

"I'm telling you this because…" She trailed off. Scottie looked at her. "Because, I'm pregnant."

"What?" Scottie leaped on to Tara, hugging her. "Are you serious?"

Tara nodded, her face in Scottie's hair. Now Tara was crying, her words muffled in Scottie's hair. "I'm pregnant, and Brett doesn't want anything to do with it."

"No!" Scottie pulled back, looking into her friend's face, anger filling her up where the sadness had been moments ago. "Are you kidding me?"

Tara's eyes watered.

Scottie wanted to wring Brett's neck. Her hate for him came to full fruition. "I've never liked him. I always thought he was such a loser. He didn't deserve you at all." Scottie's words spilled like water from a faucet no longer denied to run free. "You deserved so much better than him, the dumbass! I can't believe he would just walk away like this! From you and his unborn child!"

The pain of Scottie's childhood came back. She'd been the result of a one-night stand. Like Brett, her father hadn't wanted anything to do with a child. Her parents had both been only twenty years old and from very different worlds. Thank God her grandmother had stayed in touch.

"Scott?" Tara's voice brought her back to the present. "This is what I'm trying to tell you…"

Scottie shook her head, not understanding anything. Or understanding and refusing to acknowledge it. "What?"

Sighing deeply, Tara grabbed Scottie's hand and held it tight. "Good men are few and far between. God, I hate that saying. My mom always said that. But, really, I think Konrad is one of the few good ones."

"But—"

"I know what he did, and I know what he was. I

mean, he was a total playboy. Check social media. A lot of women wanted a chance at him. But what he did … the way he basically laid himself at your feet not once, but twice, and in front of people … he's a good one." Tara released Scottie's hand. "Don't forget that just because of your hurt pride. Which really is what? Nothing. It's your way to protect yourself from getting hurt. But you can't. Not if you want to fall in love and get married. I know you do."

"The list…"

"Screw the list! Who cares about that list? You know why? You were last on it, right?" Scottie nodded as Tara continued. "You were last on that list, and I don't think there has been anyone else since you."

Scottie was beside herself. "I don't know…" It was more than she could emotionally handle.

Tara stood, looking as frustrated as Scottie felt. "Whatever. I just wanted to let you know that."

Scottie slumped back down on the bed, pulling her phone from under the pillow once Tara was gone and she was alone again. She scrolled through Konrad's last text messages.

Konrad: **I'm coming for you. I hope you are ready for me.**

Konrad: **Scottie, please answer the phone. I need to talk to you.**

Konrad: **Baby, I know why you are mad. Can you please talk?**

Konrad: **Scottine, I'm sorry. Hear me out.**

Konrad: **Please let me explain. I love you.**

The last message was from last night, after the party fiasco.

Konrad: **I'm sorry I disappointed you. But you also disappointed me.**

Her gaze moved up one, to the last text from

Thursday night. **Please let me explain. I love you.** How did that message get lost in everything else? Too late now.

****

Two weeks later October had come around finally, and Scottie browsed the Internet for jobs. It was Monday, prime time for job searching. She had been unemployed since Korr Properties and just couldn't go back to the agency. She'd lied to them anyway.

So many things she'd do differently. She felt as if she'd aged two years and not two weeks. She hadn't really been unemployed, though. She'd helped Tara with the catering business by booking appointments, invoicing, doing inventory, and the like. She'd also still helped serve and prepare the menu several times since Konrad's surprise birthday party. Tara's business was really taking off, which was wonderful. The plan was to work until the baby came in seven months.

"You should just work for me." Tara's voice came from behind.

"No. Thanks, though." Scottie wasn't a good assistant. She needed a job where she could make decisions and have a role with authority.

"Or…" Tara paused, pulling out a chair across the dining table from Scottie, who continued to scan openings. "You can be my partner? I mean, you have a business degree. You can manage the business side of things."

Scottie looked up. "Really? Your partner?"

Tara beamed. "Yeah. You've been so good with the money part of Decadent Chick. I don't think I would be getting this successful if it wasn't for you."

What a compliment! Scottie's eyes moved to the computer screen again. *Why not?* It seemed like the next logical step. And she loved working with Tara, despite everything. She could help build the catering business for Tara and the baby. It could be their legacy.

Just as she was about to give Tara an ecstatic yes, her gaze moved over an ad that caught her attention.

ASSISTANT BREWERS WANTED

New microbrewery now hiring. Inquire on-site.

Scottie read the address listed. *The EaDo property.* Konrad had sold the property to the Bayou Sling!

Oh, God.

Scottie stood from the chair, knocking a stack of catering invoices to the floor. She couldn't explain the rush inside her to act. It was primal. It was what she needed. Nothing could stop her, not her pride or her stupid what-ifs, from taking the plunge. And for the first time, she wasn't afraid of where she would land.

Chapter Thirty-Five

Konrad held the Renee Lalique brooch. He'd not sold it back to Space City Pawn and didn't want to. He knew, however, that he couldn't keep it. How would he get it back to Scottie? He didn't think he could see her again. It was too painful.

It was Monday, and his new temp had started his second week with him. It was a guy just out of college. Fine with him. Konrad decided he was off women for a while. A long while. He still tasted Scottie on his lips. No one could replace the flavor. If this was love, it was truly the worst thing that could happen to a man.

Konrad set the box back in the drawer he'd kept it in since his birthday disaster. Actually, "disaster" was too mild a word for what had happened. He was sure his friends were keeping an eye on him, just in case he was contemplating jumping off the Korr Corp building.

They were too dramatic. Why hadn't any of those wankers coddled Fabian when he thought he'd lost Antonia to Stephan? This would not make Konrad weak. This would make him strong—stronger for the next time.

Whenever that would be.

A knock on his door took him from his reverie. Good. He needed to think about something else for a while. He looked up from his desk. Groaning, he saw Jeff on the other side of the door, looking in like a lost puppy. What the hell did he want?

Konrad waved him in, watching as he eased in with that feigned casualness he always had around Konrad. "Jeff. Fancy seeing you here on the twenty-fifth floor."

He walked with caution to Konrad's colossal desk. "I thought I'd ask about getting a temp for the software team while I interview candidates. We are totally back-logged with data entry and debugging."

Konrad steepled his fingers, pressing the point into his chin. "You know I don't get involved with human resource affairs for Properties or Solutions."

Jeff looked uncomfortable.

"Sit down. You look like something's on your mind. And it's not about a new temp, is it?" Konrad watched him. He might know what was on his mind.

"Scottie left the job so quickly, I didn't know if something was wrong with her."

There it was. Konrad did his best not to move a muscle or make a sound. He didn't want to show how much he missed her. How much her absence affected him.

"She moved on. It's not unusual for temps to leave, Jeff." His voice shook a bit, but no one would notice. He hoped.

Jeff shook his head. "Right."

He was silent for too long, long enough for it to get awkward. Konrad released his hands to the desk, done with the conversation. "Is there anything else?"

"I saw you." Jeff's eyes caught Konrad's. They were defiant, filled with loathing.

"Pardon?" Konrad's body sparked with energy. This might end badly. He needed to be careful.

"At H Bar. I saw you and Scottie in the hall by the bathrooms." His stare grew more intense, more knowing, and Konrad got it. Jeff obviously thought Konrad had crossed a line. Used her and made her leave.

"I don't know what you're suggesting, Jeff—"

"You sexually harassed her, didn't you? And that's why she left." He spat out the words in disgust.

Rage filled Konrad. If he wasn't at risk of losing everything, he'd reach over the desk and take Jeff by the throat. He'd already been emotionally charged, and this was a slap in the face. His own employee thought this about him? That he was capable of sexually harassing another employee? That was the one line he'd never cross. Ever. Scottie was different. Scottie was a woman he wanted to keep and not just have a dalliance with. And she wasn't his employee.

Konrad turned to his phone. "Perhaps we need to get legal and human resources in here so they can hear your accusation? Because there has never once been such a claim made since I began Korr Corporation."

The glass door burst open hard enough that Konrad thought the whole damn wall would come down in shards. He jumped up from his chair, as did Jeff.

Scottie.

She stood, her chest heaving, her eyes wild as she stood in the doorway. Dressed in jeans and a t-shirt, she looked as if she'd just rolled out of bed. Konrad didn't know what to say. What to think. There were too many thoughts and too many feelings churning inside him.

"You said you loved me in that text," she began in a surprisingly steady voice, considering the condition she was in. One step in front of the other, she made her way across his office, completely ignoring the fact that Jeff had been there too. "Did you mean it?"

Konrad's heart pounded in his chest, and he was back at his fateful party. He was back at the place where he was on his knees for her, and she had rejected him callously. Yes, he loved her, dammit, but he didn't love this. He didn't love her intrusion on him when he was trying to get on. In his office. His bread and butter. She had no right to come in and make him beg for her again.

"Jeff, please leave now." Konrad didn't want another scene. He was tired of them. Exhausted of them.

"*Now* you want some privacy?" Her eyes blazed,

challenging him.

"Jeff," Konrad said again, stronger. He wasn't asking. He was demanding. Jeff didn't move though. "Get out, Jeff!"

With that final demand, Jeff leaped to the door, getting out of their way. The door snapped shut, and Konrad could see from his periphery that Susan and other employees were standing outside. Another crowd.

"You can't come into my office demanding me, Scottie," he said coolly, but his heart was melting. She had tears in her eyes.

"I know you sold the EaDo property to Bayou Sling."

"So?" How much he wanted to go to her, to take her in his arms. Kiss her again. It had been too long since his lips had touched hers, but he could practically feel them as she stood there, watching her mouth.

"Why?" Her voice quivered, as did her lips.

He shrugged. "I had a change of heart." *Did you?* He wanted to ask her but couldn't. He didn't want to know.

"So easy?" She choked on her question.

He choked on his answer. "No."

"Then why?" She wasn't going to let it go, and he just wanted her to leave. Her presence affected him too much. He couldn't be rejected by her again.

He scrubbed his face. "I don't see why this is important for you to know."

"I see why. Tell me. Why did you sell the EaDo property to Bayou Sling?"

He lifted his clenched fists in exasperation. "Because you were right. Because it wasn't about profit. It was about community, about building something long-term. About doing the right thing. Okay? Is that what you want me to admit?"

He couldn't look at her anymore.

He dropped his gaze to the floor. "Why are you here, Scottie? It's over, remember?"

The air grew thick, tense. He thought he'd suffocate if the silence lasted any longer.

"I've never understood love from a man, not from a young age. My dad didn't want anything to do with me. I don't know where he is. I never really knew. When I saw that hook-up list, I felt like I was my mother, and I always told myself I would never be like her. I would never let a man hurt me. Because that was my childhood. I couldn't believe you because I was afraid of giving you my love and you destroying it because of who I thought you were. Maybe I destroyed myself instead. But you have to tell me, did you mean what you said in that text?"

"Scottie," Konrad said on a sigh, his heart so full it weighed him down. "Stop this."

Her tears fell then. "I love you, Konrad. And I came to see if you still love me. And I'm not afraid of your answer."

"Jesus, Scottie," he said, his voice gaining more strength.

"Just say it. Just tell me once and for all, so I can put this behind me."

"Fuck."

"Can't you tell me?"

"Yes! I fucking love you, Scottine!" he yelled, his voice booming through his office. "You are the only woman I've ever felt love for. The only woman I've ever wanted to change for. But you can't come here after everything and demand my heart. You can't!"

"You mean the way *you* demanded mine?" Tears gushed from her eyes, wetting her t-shirt.

Slowly, and with more control than he had to give, he said, "Leave."

She gasped, obviously stunned, as was he, by that word.

Scottie wiped her face, nodding. "Okay. I'm sorry. I'm sorry I disappointed you." She turned toward the door, her steps slow.

Fuck. His heart burst inside him. He closed his eyes, every moment they shared coming in flashes. No, this wasn't right. He opened his eyes, his whole body sparking with energy. With urgency, he moved to the door just before she pulled the door handle and spun her around. She gasped.

"Don't you fucking doubt me again." With those words, he put his hands on her face and crashed his mouth on hers in a hungry kiss. He was starved for her, and she matched his intensity.

When they parted, he wiped her tears. She wiped his.

He pressed his forehead against hers. "You have to trust me. Trust that you have my loyalty. My heart."

She hugged him tight, her heart thumping so hard he felt it. "I trust you, Konrad, with everything. With my everything."

"Good. Because I want to wake up with you, and I want you to bring an overnight bag. And I want you in my future." Words he'd never thought he'd utter to another person.

He pulled back to get a good look at his woman and smiled, taking in every curve of her face. He knew, without a doubt, he was in love.

The End

EVERNIGHT PUBLISHING ®

www.evernightpublishing.com